MOVE ON BUNNY!

Published by
Prakash Books India Pvt. Ltd.
113/A, Darya Ganj,
New Delhi-110 002
Tel: (011) 2324 7062 – 65, Fax: (011) 2324 6975
Email: info@prakashbooks.com/sales@prakashbooks.com

ISBN: 978 81 7234 388 0

Processed & printed in India

MOVE ON BUNNY!

VIVEK ATRAY

Fifty years of public service...have only increased his balance, open-mindedness, sanity and humorous appreciation of the quaint human spectacle.

Paramahansa Yogananda's words on Mahatma Gandhi in the spiritual classic, *Autobiography of a Yogi.*

Acknowledgements

When writing a humorous account, the writer is greatly boosted by the presence of people of cheer around him. I would like to acknowledge the following persons who, by dint of just being who they are, have contributed towards the making of this fun-filled book:

God.

My parents and grandparents, who are no longer with us, but who continue to bless me and us.

My lovely wife, Neena, for being her very loveable self.

My daughters, Spriha and Kavya, for being the sweetest and brightest girls.

Rajesh Markanda, the busy lawyer, for fracturing his foot just in time to go through my first draft in detail and make invaluable suggestions.

Dr. Rajan Shonek and my sisters, the beautiful twins, Suruchi and Surabhi, for their love and support, always.

Ramona for designing the cover so imaginatively, Sona for being so creative, and Jujhar for his suggestions; little Angad too!

My in-laws, Mr. D. R. Sood and Mrs. Usha Sood, for their everlasting blessings.

My uncles and aunts, cousins, nephews and nieces and other relatives, all of them, for their life-long encouragement.

My friends, Sunil, Dr. Naresh, Prof. Rajnish, Dr. Sanjay, and many more, each one of them, for just being my friends.

Taru Bahl and Aamit Khanna, my advisors, for their invaluable suggestions.

My publisher, Shikha Sabharwal, for being ever-buoyant and for sticking to deadlines!

My editor, Sonalini, for her incisive and qualitative inputs.

Thank you all, for being who you are, and for being people of cheer!

1

Hot Stuff Bunny!

It was all over his face! Bunny Kapoor was shaken up. He had seen it coming, but had been too slow to react. He was not particularly used to having squishy-squashy food items thrown at him with great velocity. The missile had hit him squarely on the nose, spreading across his face while emitting the unmistakable aroma of spaghetti in fresh tomato sauce. A few sniggers were audible in the room, and he noticed a pretty looking girl giving him a very amused look. Not good! Without attempting to identify his assailant at that particular time, he vanished into the washroom lest too many people notice his plight.

He emerged shortly, looking more like the prim and proper manager of *Hot Stuff* restaurant that he was. The only noticeable difference being that his normally charming smile had been replaced with a frown. Bunny Kapoor was not one to let such an affront go unanswered. But no sooner had he traced the origins of the flying dish to table number 15-A that the horror of it all dawned upon him. It was Polly!

She glared at poor Bunny scornfully and, as he stood there open-mouthed and wide-eyed gaping at her, she flung another missile at him—a glass of mango milk shake—that caught him in mid-stare.

Now, Bunny was an ardent fan of mangoes. He literally craved them! But not when they'd conspired with a milky fluid and with his ex-girlfriend to spoil his recently washed countenance and also his new coat's collar. He hated mangoes at such times. In fact, the manner in which the gooey stuff was now dripping onto his clothes felt so horribly uncomfortable that he let out a cry.

'Ahhh!' he exclaimed. 'Look what you've done now, Polly! You've ruined my new coat!'

'And you have ruined my life, you imposter!' was the loud and clear response from the lissom lass. People at the other tables turned to look at the warring twosome.

'I'd never wanted to see you again in my life but, here you are, walking around in my favourite restaurant as if you own the place! The moment I set my eyes on you, my blood boiled!' Polly continued with her tirade.

Bunny Kapoor was endowed with an intelligent brain that worked efficiently at most times, and this was definitely one such time. It did not take him long to realize that his was easily the weaker position of the two quarrelling parties, and that the whole restaurant was at that moment probably in the process of deciding to side with his ex. He also noticed that another bowl containing hot spaghetti still adorned Polly's table and, while he was aware that *Hot Stuff's* spaghetti was among the best in the land, he also knew that a woman whose blood was self-admittedly boiling would not hesitate to throw it at him. Especially, given her most recent past record.

Discretion being the better part of valour, Bunny withdrew once more to the washroom with the haste of one who wouldn't have done too badly at the 50 metres dash. In fact, Bunny had been an outstanding athlete at his alma mater, Cambridge High School, situated in the periphery of New Delhi, and had won many medals as well as some hearts there. But, at that moment, he was in a state of bewildered anxiety. His clothes were badly soiled, and he could also distinctly hear the shrill voice of the young woman at table 15-A, who was in the process of relating details of their breezy romance to the listeners in the hall. Polly certainly knew how to get her point across effectively, recalled Bunny. He pondered upon possible ways to get out of his predicament while standing in the slightly smelly confines of the washroom. Bunny had many inherent attributes and the ability to pick up smells which normally escaped the notice of most others was one of them.

'I must remember to pull up the cleaning agency,' was the thought that came to the mind of the diligent Manager of *Hot Stuff* even at that moment of personal crisis.

Bunny realized that he had two options. To either brave it and walk out once again thereby risking attack from not just the fearsome spaghetti-thrower but also maybe from onlookers possibly moved to violence by Polly's sordid (one-sided!) tale. Or to stay put.

Deciding in favour of the latter, Bunny remained holed up in the smelly loo until the cacophony subsided and then left for home directly after mumbling something into the ear of his number-two, Nippy Singh.

Bunny realized later, as he settled into his bean bag, wanting it to engulf him completely, that even Nippy had looked highly amused at the situation. What if he went and told the story to Mr. Singh, the owner!

'I'll surely lose my job,' thought Bunny, for Mr. Singh was not known to take the phenomenon of food items flying about in his restaurant lightly.

He sank deeper and deeper into his bean-bag and into realms of despair with each dreadful thought. The precise moment when Bunny fell asleep remains unknown to mankind till this day.

Bunny Kapoor was handsome, tallish, clean shaven and short-haired. He was always in perfect shape, even without trying too hard. He dressed well, mostly in blues and greys, and spoke fluently. It did not take much effort for him to impress people. It came naturally to him.

As a student, he had never been outstanding in any particular field, but then he'd never craved to be. We have already learnt that the sports-field was an exception to this rule. He had scorched the school tracks on many occasions and his parents had noted with pride that the number of trophies in his closet had kept swelling. In addition to this, Bunny was also adept at setting the dance floor afire when he wanted to.

Since his childhood, Bunny had been a likeable, pleasant, happy-go-lucky kind of fellow. His friends adored him; even his enemies admitted that he was not a bad sort. The only two species of people with whom he tended to fall foul were former girlfriends and current bosses.

Bunny had spent his early life in the outskirts of New Delhi and had always been in awe of the big bad Metro. His father had been a banker, and his mother a teacher. Both had now retired and had settled in Noida, near Delhi.

Once he landed his first job and then his first metro girlfriend, Bunny's self-confidence grew. Thereafter, he took on Delhi and the challenges it posed head on. Bunny felt that he was now in a winning position. He just had to cruise along life's pathways in much the same way. He had joined the restaurant, *Hot Stuff,* in Vasant Vihar, a posh area of South Delhi, about a month ago, after having changed several jobs in various parts of the city. He and Polly fell out at about the same time.

Polly had been a lively girlfriend. They had got along well and had spent some really out-there evenings together. During the course of their meetings at the Adventure Café, he had often looked deeply into her eyes and had told her, as he had told a few others before her, that she was the most beautiful girl in the world. It's not that he lied at such times. It's just that each time he looked into the eyes of a beautiful girl, he felt from the core of his heart that she was indeed God's most gorgeous creation. And, as everyone knows, there has never been a dearth of beautiful girls in New Delhi.

She, in turn, had seemed quite fond of him, but their short-lived romance had crash-landed when she discovered that he had been involved with other women before her! Our truthful hero had himself told her all in a moment of weakness, and that had been that.

As for bosses, they come in all shapes, sizes and temperaments. They also come in a wide variety of behavioural styles: some are the suspicious sorts, others are over-ambitious, and still others are balding dictators. Bunny's bosses had been a cocktail of all these and he knew that he could never stand their tantrums for long. He was ever-ready to move on to another assignment. At present, though, despite his very *bossy* boss, he wished to stick to his job at *Hot Stuff*, and there was a very special reason for that.

When he arrived for work the next morning, Bunny was greeted by faces that looked familiar but which had abnormally wide smiles pasted across them. In fact, each employee of the restaurant sported one such smile.

'What's so funny?' wondered Bunny, as he settled into his chair and switched on his laptop.

Suddenly sensing that something was amiss, he got up and stared into the tiny mirror that adorned his cabin's wall. His attractive face stared intently back at him. Bunny was not fair, but his countenance was well sculpted and he looked younger than his 25 years. His tie was straight and there was not even any sign of gooey stuff on his face. He looked good! Then why was the staff so amused?

Determined to find out *immédiatement,* Bunny rushed towards Nippy, his aforementioned number-two. The latter still had the same look on his face that Bunny had left him with the previous afternoon.

Bunny wondered whether it was all part of a sinister plan.

'Well?' was his direct and succinct poser to Nippy.

'Mr. Singh wants us to re-enact the throwing scene from yesterday,' Nippy was clearly unable to control his mirth.

'Re-enact?? You mean the spaghetti and mango-shake throwing incident? Why on earth…?'

Before he could add to his list of hastily delivered counter questions, Bunny saw from the corner of his eye that the boss himself had entered the room.

Shekhar Singh was not a tall man and was not well built either. He sported a small moustache and, in fact, had a rather nondescript look. He had such an aggressive demeanour, however, with a booming voice to match, that he intimidated most earthly beings. Two such beings now turned to greet the owner of *Hot Stuff*.

'Kapoor, I understand that there was a pie-throwing incident here yesterday?' he asked his manager.

'Pies?' thought Bunny, without uttering a word. 'There were no pies. There was mango-shake and before that there was spaghetti, but no pies. Pies were thrown about in the days of Laurel and Hardy!' he recalled.

'WELL?' was the one-word, eardrum-shattering bit of interrogation from Mr. Singh.

'No, sir...Yes, sir…' was all Bunny could mumble, as Mr. Singh gave him a real firing, admonishing him for various shortcomings in his character including the gravest lapse of having had a girlfriend in the first place, and then having dumped her in the second.

'So now we will have a re-enactment!' concluded Mr. Singh as he stomped over to table 15-A, followed by an entourage of chefs and waiters. They all looked distinctly excited at the prospect of the ensuing drama.

'I want to know exactly what happened so that I can prevent such goings-on in future! This is where she was seated, I am told?'

He did not wait for a response and plonked himself onto a chair at table 15-A, which, as Bunny noted with some trepidation, was once again adorned with tomato spaghetti and mango-shake!

'What a crazy choice of menu!' thought Bunny to himself,

thereby getting even with both his ex girlfriend and his present boss in one stroke, though only in his mind.

He didn't see it coming this time either. It was all over his face. As gooey and as sticky as it had been the previous day. The only difference being that Mr. Singh threw the mango shake at him immediately thereafter, without a pause. He was about to fire some more spaghetti but checked his throw. Bunny saw from an uncovered corner of his eye that Mr. Singh's gorgeous daughter had walked into the hall. Mr. Singh gave his progeny a sheepish look and proceeded to tuck into the spaghetti as if he had meant to do so all along!

Readers would recall that Bunny had a very special reason for sticking to his present job, despite all obstacles. That reason now stood before him in all her glory.

Alankrita Singh was quite a woman! If she had any flaw, it was not easily discernable. Tall and lissom, she was blessed with a flawless complexion, a voice that was music to the ears, and as if that was not enough, she was also endowed with a brilliant mind. She had given up a lucrative job with a renowned consulting firm in the US in order to help her father expand his business. She was eager and enthusiastic about everything she did.

Bunny Kapoor, his face covered with gooey food-stuff, gaped at the dazzling new entrant.

'Well?' was the question that she posed to her father.

Bunny had heard that one before. It seemed to be a popular question for the Singh family members to ask each other, as also for the manager-level employees of their restaurant to ask their juniors. The look on Mr. Singh's face was an unfamiliar one for Bunny though. It was a look that mixed fear with embarrassment and even a bit of love. Quite unique it was, especially when it represented the exterior of such a fearsome personality. In no mood to answer his daughter's query, Mr. Singh gave the impression that he had never been hungrier in his life and polished off the spaghetti in quick time before finally turning his face upward to speak.

'My darling daughter, there you are! I was just sampling the ware. I must keep the staff on their toes you know.'

'Dad...why is this man standing here with spaghetti sliding down his face?'Alankrita demanded of him.

'My dear, I haven't the foggiest idea. Come with me! Let's go and take a look at the site where we're planning to set up our new restaurant. Don't bother your precious head with trivial matters!' said Mr. Singh, as he got up and walked out without answering her question.

Alankrita Singh opened her pretty mouth as if to ask another question but decided against it and ended up directing a quizzical look towards Bunny before following her Dad towards the exit.

Bunny gazed at her with the uncovered portion of his eye as she left. He experienced mixed feelings at that moment. Her very presence had quickened the pace of his heartbeat, but her ignorance of his identity was dampening. He had met her only twice earlier, and briefly at that. Bunny had been sure that she had liked the way he looked. But, by referring to him as "this man", Alankrita had poured cold water over his dreams. He did feel better though when he realised that it would have clearly been difficult for her to recognize him with his face barely visible through all that unwarranted camouflage.

Not a man to be put down easily, Bunny proceeded to direct a fierce one-eyed look towards the members of the staff, all of whom were still grinning at his misfortune. Their smiles vanished abruptly as a result of his glare, and so did Bunny once more to the confines of the smelly washroom, his ego damaged and bruised, but not shattered. He was determined to get his own back on Mr. Singh, and to also win over his gorgeous daughter, come what may.

Having become an expert by now at cleaning up his face quickly despite several layers of deposit accumulating upon it, Bunny walked out of the washroom within a minute, strode straight across the hall and out into the garden to join Mr. Singh and Alankrita.

Father and daughter were at the time animatedly discussing the site visible in its entirety over a short wooden fence that served as the boundary of the premises. There was obviously an argument on, and the father of the beauty was clearly not winning it. Alankrita was shouting out aloud while he was just being able to manage to get in a word here and there. She seemed adamant upon converting the site into a spa resort with a small eatery while he was evidently in favour of establishing a large Chinese restaurant.

As Bunny approached them, quite fearlessly for one so recently under attack from one of them, they turned to look at him. Bunny's attention was focused upon Alankrita, as can be expected under the circumstances, but he had not expected her to drop her jaw on finally recognising him.

'Oh my God!' she exclaimed. 'Were you the one with that stuff on your face in there?'

'Yes indeed, Ma'am, it was me,' responded our man, without diverting his gaze from her angelic face.

'Good God, Dad! You threw food on the face of your manager! I didn't recognize him in there. Poor, Bunny!'

The adjective 'poor' has many connotations but, in this case, Bunny was sure that she had utilized it to indicate her fondness for him. Her words had been uttered in a voice that matched the tone of one who was used to getting her point across, but to Bunny's ears, her words were sheer music. Also, the manner in which his name had been uttered and the fact that it had emanated from those lovely lips made Bunny feel that his name had never sounded quite so beautiful. Feeling heady at this happy turn of events, Bunny turned to look at his boss for the first time since intruding upon the duo.

Shekhar Singh was seldom in a good mood. And, at this moment, his blood pressure seemed to be on the rise in a hurry. He gave 'poor Bunny' a really ugly glare and was about to open his mouth when the music started once again. Alankrita started speaking.

'Dad! Don't you dare glare at Bunny like that! I thought you'd given up that look altogether after Mamma walked out on you for using it on her.'

The fact that this private bit of information had just been made public by his daughter had a dramatic effect on Shekhar Singh. He turned a combination of pink, red and blue and started fuming at the ears. Bunny was sure that his boss was about to explode, but it was also clear that he was terrified enough of his daughter to refrain from any violence. Mr. Singh, a decisive man, abruptly decided to quit the scene, for he knew that he was in a no-win situation.

Bunny knew that this was the moment he'd been waiting for. He took a very quick deep breath and, before Alankrita could even utter another word, he blurted out his request.

'Ma'am, may I take you out to dinner tonight in order to suggest some ideas that I have for the spa resort that you are contemplating? I know a classy little place in Hauz Khas.'

There! He'd said it now and there was no going back. She would either fire him for his impudence or she would see merit in his idea. The look on her glorious visage was one of surprise, followed by one of shock and then by one of amusement. She smiled at him and opened her mouth to speak, while his heart fluttered rapidly.

'Actually, I should not accept your invitation for two reasons. One, you eavesdropped on the conversation that I was having with my Dad and are now trying to butt into a private matter. Two, you have no experience of working in spas or anything remotely resembling them if one goes by your resume, a copy of which is lying on my table. But, I like the spark in your eye and I want to hear what you have to say. So pick me up at 8 o'clock. If you're late, you're dead!'

With that pronouncement, and with a flourish that was almost too much for Bunny to bear, she sailed away towards her spanking new red sports car. She zoomed off as more than one onlooker gaped, and was probably touching 90 kilometres an hour within 3 seconds! The Delhi Police would not know what hit them, thought Bunny.

He almost fell to the ground! Oh, how his head was spinning! This latest turn of events was proving a bit too much for him to handle, and he was thrilled to bits!

Bunny had grabbed the moment, seized the initiative, belled the cat and struck when the iron was hot! By inviting Alankrita Singh to dinner, he had shown himself to be the sort of man who could take on a dozen fearsome beasts in one bare-handed battle. Alankrita Singh was so intimidating, blessed as she was with a deadly combination of looks, class, and brains, that no man had ever quite had the guts to try and get close to her. But Bunny Kapoor had floored her with one stroke. Or so he thought. He knew that he had a chance with her. She had had a definite gleam in her eye when accepting his invitation. He had met enough girls in his life to recognize that look with certainty. And the fact that she still had his résumé on her table!

'Wow!' thought Bunny. 'Now why would she do that, if not to know all she can about me? And if Mr. Singh's darling daughter has taken a liking to me, the tyrant would have no choice but to go soft on me!'

Feeling rather upbeat at his current situation, Bunny Kapoor dashed into the restaurant and started planning for the evening. It was sure to be one of the most significant ones of his life…

The next morning, the staff of *Hot Stuff* was not sure how to react to their manager's behaviour. Ever since reporting to work, Bunny had been behaving quite unpredictably. One moment he would come up to one of them and put his arm around his shoulder to enquire about his personal well-being and the next moment he would be shouting at the same hapless junior for no apparent reason at all. Sitting at his own desk now, Bunny himself was not sure whether to scream with happiness or to collapse in despair. It had been *that* sort of evening.

It had started well enough.

He had taken special care to groom himself adequately for the date. A quick look in the mirror had confirmed that he was looking all suave and dapper. Just the look he had been aiming for! He had worn his best jacket with an attractive shirt and a dazzling tie to match. There was no doubt that he was at his very best. He knew he had to be.

He had arrived five minutes early at the door of his boss's palatial house in Green Park and, despite knowing well the potential perils of bumping into him, he had taken a deep breath and rung the bell. To his pleasant surprise, it was the angel herself who appeared and he was attacked by another bout of giddiness. She was looking looked like a dream—again. He almost forgot to hand over the red carnations that he had bought for her.

After recovering his poise—a few seconds after doing an open mouthed fish act—he took her arm and they walked to his car.

'We can't go in that!' Alankrita had exclaimed in disdain on approaching the modest second-hand convertible that Bunny had bought the previous year. He had been rather proud of it uptil now.

The lady pulled out her own car's keys from a snazzy designer-labelled white handbag that went well with her shimmering dress. The keys were those of the same car of zip-zap-zoom fame; it was standing right next to his own car, and was making it look like a rickshaw.

'Hop in!' she said to him as she jumped into it with amazing athleticism. Bunny had just made it to the passenger's seat when she sped off, her companion hanging on for dear life! Despite the odds, he managed to keep his wits about him. He played navigator all the way to the designated restaurant in the busy Hauz Khas locality. The place was buzzing with people out for a good time. Finding a parking slot was tough, but they were not to be denied and, before long, they were walking towards their destination. They found a table by the window and Alankrita was immediately in her element. The awestruck Bunny could only look and listen. Instead of allowing Bunny to advise her about the Spa, as had been the plan, she proceeded to give him a long lecture on the latest trends in the hospitality sector.

Bunny Kapoor sat transfixed, gazing at her and listening to her nightingale-like voice. The effect that her close proximity had upon him is difficult to describe. She was so captivating that, before long, he found himself floating on a dreamy cloud of bliss. The food on their table had only been incidental, so engrossed had they been in their respective pursuits at the time. Bunny even visualized himself at the ripe old age of 65 with Alankrita by his side as his wife of several decades, surrounded by their toddler-grandchildren. She still looked beautiful, though a little plump and he looked just as handsome, though his hairline had receded and he wore reading glasses. It was no surprise then that, after a while, Alankrita realized that her companion was not listening to her at all.

'Did you hear what I just said, Bunny? Did you? You seem to be lost somewhere. You haven't been listening to me! Come on, repeat what I've been saying!' she demanded of him.

Bunny had been confronted by several calamitous situations in his life. And knew instinctively, as his reverie ended quite abruptly, that this was surely one such. In fact, for all he knew, his very future depended substantially upon his next few words. The problem was that he didn't have a clue about what she'd been saying. Now, if he, by some divine miracle, were to answer her query with a close-to-reality statement, then the contents of his reverie had some chance of coming true. On the other hand, if his guess was off-the-mark, he could bid her goodbye forever!

'Dash it! Why didn't I listen to her carefully!' he thought, cursing himself. He was drowning in deepening gloom.

The fierce look in her dazzling eyes dented his confidence further. She seemed ready to box him if need be! The Delhi crowd seated in the vicinity would have been highly amused if that were to happen. Drawing upon hitherto unknown reservoirs of intuition within him, Bunny took a deep breath and blurted out his all-important response.

'Come on, Alankrita! Of course I was listening. You were telling me about your plan to start a health café,' he said, red-faced.

It is not easy to understand a woman at the best of times, and this was clearly one of the worst. For some reason, the look on Alankrita's face went from being very-fierce to being ever-so-gentle in a matter of milliseconds. At first, Bunny thought that he had achieved the perfect fluke, and had accurately described what she had been lecturing him about, despite not having heard a single word of it. On looking at her face more closely, it dawned upon him that it was something else that had pleased the beauty.

'Bunny, oh Bunny! That's it. What a magnificent idea! We'll start a health café instead of a spa. Who wants a spa anyway? Dad will be pleased too. Good night, Bunny!'

Bunny realized that if *he* was being credited with the originality of the health café idea, then she had obviously been talking about something else. Alankrita had seemed to have forgiven him for not listening, apparently in recognition of his brilliant brainwave.

She proceeded there and then to slam down a thick wad of notes on the table to pay the bill, before giving Bunny a quick hug and rushing out of the place with a spring in her step. Left quite befuddled by the turn of events, and without a vehicle, Bunny had to walk all the way to Green Park to pick up his car. He had not had the gumption to ring her bell for the second time that night. He returned to his own apartment to try and sleep, but his endeavours did not meet with much success. It had all been too much for him.

Sitting at his desk this morning, as Bunny emerged from his latest day-dream, he wondered where he stood in Alankrita's eyes. He kept pondering over the possibilities. It was not long before he fell asleep, his head on his table.

When he finally awoke, it was well past noon. Most restaurant managers who sleep on the job are likely to find that much went wrong while they were doing so.

'Gosh!' he thought to himself, 'I'm surely going to lose my job for this, brilliant health-café ideas notwithstanding.'

As he rubbed his eyes, he found his boss walking in, looking exceedingly pleased about something. From his expression, it seemed that Bunny's job was safe, at least for now.

'My boy, Bunny! Congratulations!' exclaimed Mr. Singh. 'Alankrita informs me that you have come up with the most exquisite idea of a health café for our new site. I must say I'm impressed!'

Bunny stood up with an abrupt movement, much like a jack in the box, and again rubbed his eyes like a child.

'Excuse me, sir. Did I hear you correctly? I think you just congratulated me for something. May I know what that happy news is, sir?'

'Yes of course, my boy,' said Mr. Singh, thereby using the phrase 'my boy' for the second time in succession. Bunny was not used to this sort of treatment from his boss.

'You should know that I have promoted you to the post of General Manager, with immediate effect!'

So amiable did Mr. Singh look as he uttered these words, and so astounding were the words themselves, that Bunny felt like hugging the man. But then, deciding against it, he only extended a limp hand, which his boss clasped firmly and shook vigorously.

'Bunny, my boy, I must admit that I've been mistaken about you. You have potential! I'm sure that you're going to make this dream a reality. You shall henceforth work exclusively on this new project. I am also doubling your emoluments. I plan to promote Nippy to the post of Manager in your place.' Mr. Singh explained further to Bunny's delight.

The boss was keen to share more details of his grandiose plans with the new found apple of his eye and had just opened his mouth to continue when the original apple walked into the room. Alankrita! The new entrant was not one to let others take centre stage and proceeded forthwith to dominate the proceedings. Dressed in sheer blue, she resembled a Miss Universe contestant. Bunny was transfixed once more.

'Bunny! How nice to see you!' was her opening remark to him.

'Dad! What are you doing here?' was the second.

'It's so hot in here!' was the third. No one could dispute this last fact, Bunny's cabin was always 'so hot'.

Bunny noticed that Mr. Singh was in the process of making a quick escape. Soon he was nowhere to be seen; he really did seem to be awfully terrified of his daughter!

Bunny had just thought of saying something when Alankrita decided to continue with her monologue.

'Bunny, we need you to move into your new office forthwith! Come with me.'

So saying, she caught him by the arm and pulled him toward hers Dad's office chamber. Before long, they were inside the plush room, with Shekhar Singh still nowhere to be seen.

'There! Sit down, Bunny. I want to see you on that chair. Dad can shift somewhere else,' declared the mistress of proceedings with her usual flourish.

Bunny Kapoor was zapped! He sat down gingerly on the huge chair that had always intimidated him, especially at such times when it was occupied by his boss. He gradually sank into the seat and looked up at the angel-in-charge.

'I must tell you that from now on, you will work with me alone, and not with my Dad!' said the angel.

Bunny was tempted to pinch himself at this last bit of information. He had received one pleasant shock after another in the last five minutes. A promotion, accompanied by a raise! A swanky new office! And now the chance to work exclusively with Alankrita Singh, his current dream girl!

'Can I say something?' he finally managed to blurt out.

The angel did not listen. She was not used to listening. She continued with her speech.

'What we need to do is to get down to business straightaway. Formalities be damned! Let's read up some stuff on the internet and list out the bullets that would be the key to our Health Café plan, Bunny.'

Having announced her intent for the immediate future, Alankrita moved swiftly towards the computer on Bunny's new table and even before he could say 'Of course, Ma'am!' she placed one hand on his shoulder and the other on the keyboard to reach out and login.

Our hero, as we have already noted, was a courageous and resilient man. But the set of circumstances that he had encountered in the last 24 hours and the immediate proximity of Alankrita Singh, her perfume and her lithe figure, did not leave him with many options. He finally gave in and fainted.

When he was roused at last, by the unmistakable odour of mulligatawny soup, it took him a while to come to grips with his situation. As it all came back to him, Bunny smiled on realizing that he had passed out when his cup of joy had overflowed irrepressibly. Standing next to him was young Nippy, the new Manager of *Hot Stuff.* Bunny noted that he too was looking quite pleased with himself. And why not? Nippy would have had to wait for another two years in other circumstances before a raise and a promotion would have come his way. Thanks to Bunny's brainwave and the eccentricity of the Singhs, Nippy had struck gold too.

'Here, chief! Your favourite soup. Straight from the kitchen,' said Nippy.

'Nippy! How long have I been out? And where's Alankrita?' enquired Bunny, accepting the soup and taking a sip.

'Around fifteen minutes, chief! I have no clue on her whereabouts. But she did say something about telling you to call her when you got up.'

'Thanks Nippy; and by the way, congratulations on your promotion!'

'Many thanks, chief! This is all thanks to you.' Nippy smiled broadly at him.

'Nippy, my boy, the decision was all theirs. A brainwave about the health café was all that I had to offer to initiate this happy series of developments. So run along now and I'll make that call.'

'Sure, Chief. You look good in your snazzy new office!' said Nippy, as he retreated.

Taking a deep breath, Bunny dialled Alankrita's number and was about to say 'Hello!' (as is customary when you call someone up) when Alankrita's unstoppable voice continued from where it had left off. Bunny was already aware that she didn't care much for niceties.

'Bunny! Hope you had a nice nap there. Now listen! We have to go and visit some health cafés in Europe next week, so I want you to search the internet for them and make plans for a short trip. And do not forget to download some pictures along with as much information as you can on the subject. I'm so excited about this idea of yours! You're such a genius! See you later. Ciao!'

That was that. Bunny had just begun trying to assimilate the contents of that last one-way conversation when Alankrita appeared before him in flesh and blood again.

'And, Bunny, I forgot to add that Dad won't be going with us, so it'll just be you and me. Have you checked out the options yet?'

Bunny was quite breathless once more, and mumbled something about the internet, the computer and the tickets but she was gone just as suddenly as she had appeared. It was becoming a habit for her with him. It dawned upon him that Alankrita Singh was a girl who lived in the supersonic lane at all times, whether she was driving, walking or just standing. He had never seen her sitting quietly. He had never seen her with her mouth shut. He wondered how she would look at such times. She was the boss though, and, instead of pondering over her idiosyncrasies, he knew that he'd better accept or ignore them and get down to work.

Bunny looked a little like Oliver Hardy when he could finally put his feet up on returning from the Europe trip. Not that he had put on weight. He may have lost some hair along the way, but it was difficult to tell. What really made him resemble the famous man was the expression on his face. He looked distressed and perplexed. He had spent more than a hundred hours with Alankrita Singh, hitherto his dream girl, visiting beautiful locales in France, Holland and Italy. She had looked gorgeous to the hilt. He'd even had a rejuvenating massage and spent quality time in the pool. In short, he'd had the time of his life. Yet, he now felt gloomy, dull, fatigued and depressed.

As ever, Ms Singh had totally overwhelmed him. She had knocked him over, and she had floored him. She had also left him terrified. No end.

The question that was tearing his mind apart now was whether he would, after all, be able to spend a life-time with her, if Alankrita were to say yes to the proposal of marrying him. As of now, it seemed to Bunny that even a year, a month, or just a day in her company would be a bit too much. The problem was that Alankrita Singh just could not stop talking. Not for a second. Not even a microsecond! What she needed was a good listener for a husband. And to Bunny's horror, she had paid him the following compliment while gazing into his eyes, atop the Eiffel Tower, where they'd gone sightseeing: 'Oh, Bunny! You're not only brainy, you're a very good listener too. I love the way you look at me and *listen to me* as I speak.'

Sinking deeper into his bean bag, he felt dreadful at the prospect of having to listen to her for the rest of his life. He had a feeling that, should he marry her, he would be dominated by her so utterly that his life would become hell.

All of a sudden, he had a rather cheerful brainwave. He could go away and never meet her again! Even if he had to sacrifice the promotion and the new office room and the related perquisites in the bargain! The thought was sacrilegious, but it brought a smile to his face.

Bunny Kapoor was determined not to be a good listener.

2

Box Office Bunny!

Bunny Kapoor was at a loss. He was at his wit's end, in turmoil and in shock. But now, standing atop the 24-storey building, Bunny knew that he must make his move within the next 10 seconds. He took a deep breath and, without further ado, flung himself at his adversary. He landed punch after punch upon the tall man's face, surprisingly without much resistance, and as soon as he sensed that Round 1 was his, he made his next move. Running faster than he had ever done, he reached the top of the staircase and hurtled downwards, chased somewhat shakily by the enemy.

After making it down to the twenty-second floor, where the lift was available, he shot into it and pressed the 'Ground Floor' button. As the door closed, he could see his foe trying to put his shoe in, but with some deft footwork of his own, Bunny managed to keep the offending object out and the lift began its downward journey.

A pleasant looking lady got in at the fifteenth and glanced at the breathless figure a bit warily, but there was no further interruption as Bunny reached his first destination and fled thereupon to his car to drive off in haste. Only when he was three blocks down the road did Bunny relax.

He had never expected her to send a strongman to eliminate him. That was surely the man's intention, for even though he had not displayed any evidence of being armed, he had made no effort to hide his aggressive designs either. And the moment the man had uttered Kanika's name, Bunny had known that he had better flee.

Having made the foolish mistake of running up to the roof, Bunny had found himself in a tight corner with death confronting him in either of two forms—either at the thug's hands or from a fatal fall. That he'd managed to attack, escape and survive when it mattered was very brave, but he knew that he'd better tread carefully in future. His ex-girlfriends could not be taken lightly.

Bunny Kapoor felt at ease in his new job at a swanky new multiplex in Juhu, Mumbai. The bustling megapolis had been quite a change from New Delhi, which despite its capital status is a more laidback city than Mumbai and not as intense in its work culture.

As the Manager of Catalyst Multiplex, Bunny was responsible for ensuring that the ticketing, advertising and leasing of space kept the management sufficiently endowed with sufficient funds to earn profits, cater for the salaries of 200 employees and also repay debt. Already, Bunny had managed to bring in some major changes in the work environment. He had learnt the ropes quickly and had made a mark immediately. He didn't waste time in meetings. Rather, he text-messaged directives and instructions to his team-members regularly and encouraged them to text him back. Bunny had been in total command and had made it evident to the staff that he was the boss. The problem for him, as usual, was his own boss.

For one thing, Milind Sathe was Catalyst's owner's nephew, and for another, he was only 22 years old, three years younger than Bunny! These factors, plus the younger man's irksome behaviour, irritated Bunny no end.

Milind would often call Bunny up at odd hours with menial issues to resolve. He would also hold meetings frequently in which he would address Bunny as 'Kapoor' in front of the staff, a fact which infuriated Bunny.

But our man knew, as he always did, that he would one day have the last laugh, and he was biding his time. He also knew that Tarana, his deputy, was the main attraction for him at Catalyst. In order to have a chance with her, he must be patient with the boss; else he would lose his job and would then have to bid her good-bye as well.

Tarana had been named quite aptly, for she came across as nothing less than a musical composition. She traversed the distance from one end of the multiplex to the other as if she were a member of the Bolshoi Ballet, all grace and poise.

She was tall, for an Indian girl, and quite shapely. She had that air of confidence that comes naturally to girls from Mumbai. Her long black tresses and flowing dresses went well with her artistic movements. When she walked by, the boys in the coffee-shop, whether sipping coffee, or selling it, would gasp and sigh. So would the cleaning boys, the ticket-counter chaps and the youngsters queuing up to enter the theatre. The reaction of the older men was not much different either.

For Bunny Kapoor, the new Manager of Catalyst Multiplex,

Juhu, Mumbai, Tarana signified what might be referred to as the-stuff-that-dreams-are-currently-made-of.

There was just one obstacle. It was that Milind guy again. He and Tarana were batchmates from college and had evidently been close friends there. Bunny was not sure whether they were seeing each other as of now, but as was his wont, he was determined to pin down the opposition and win over the fair damsel's affections, whatever the odds.

'Come in, Kapoor,' said Milind Sathe, as Bunny walked into the room of the General Manager one day with a frown on his face.

'What is the issue at hand, Kapoor, why the grimace across your countenance?' asked Milind, who had been educated at an old-world school in England and who often used the most flowery sentences to express himself.

'For one thing, sir, I wish you would stop calling me 'Kapoor', for I'm not comfortable being called that,' responded Bunny.

'Alright, alright, Kapoor, I'll try and remember that,' said Milind, without batting an eyelid. 'And what else seems to be the bother with you this fine morning?'

Bunny glared at Milind long enough to make the other realize that he was piqued but not long enough to annoy him.

'Tarana hasn't come to work today,' said Bunny, finally. 'And I can't do without her,' he added, thereby stating a fact.

'Ah, I know the answer to that one, old boy. Today happens to be the anniversary of the day when the angelic Tarana chose to descend onto our planet earth twenty-one years ago,' explained Milind, with poetic flourish that annoyed Bunny even more.

Bunny was upset at the fact that the verbose oaf knew that it was Tarana's birthday, whereas Bunny himself had been utterly clueless about it.

'In fact, she and I are planning to meet for luncheon this afternoon,' added the boss, for good effect.

This last bit of information was quite a blow to our hero's morale, and he mumbled something to himself before leaving the beaming Milind Sathe standing near his office desk.

For some reason, Bunny was rather sure that his scheming boss had figured out that he was attracted to Tarana. Being the spoilt rich child that he was, Milind was now out to prove his supremacy over Bunny in the arena of romance as well, having already assumed the lead role over him in the professional space.

Feeling very low, Bunny walked back to his own desk and sat down to try and grasp the horrible implications of it all. His new fantasy-girl was going around with his pest-like boss. Nothing could be worse!

Strange are the ways of fate though. Just ten minutes later, Bunny walked into Milind's room once again, this time with a broad smile on his face. The latter, who had looked so pleased with himself a short while back, was the one with the frown on his face now.

'Oh no, Tarana!' Milind was shouting into his handphone.

Not realizing that his subordinate had entered the room and was now standing just a few steps away, Milind continued in a very pained tone.

'Then I'm definitely opting out!' he declared emphatically, with the air of a toddler who doesn't want to play with his friends any more.

Bunny Kapoor wondered whether to interrupt the argument or to let it continue. Surely, such arguments are not good for the health of relationships between former classmates, he realized. But the gentleman in him took over the moment he recalled that it is bad manners to eavesdrop. He coughed loudly enough for the whining Milind to look up from the phone and to realise that Bunny had been privy to the conversation, albeit only to one side of it.

'How dare you come in like this, Kapoor, without knocking?' said Milind, forgetting that Tarana was listening at the other end.

Bunny knew in a flash that his moment had come.

Raising his voice just enough for the caller at the other end of Milinds's phone to hear, Bunny stated the facts as they stood.

'I found an invitation from Tarana on my desk for the luncheon to which you were referring, sir. And so did a dozen other members of the staff, it seems, sir,' said Bunny, sounding like the lyrical Milind himself.

'You invited the whole office, did you? I thought it was to be just you and me!' screamed Milind into the phone.

'I'm not coming, and that's final!'

A musical voice could be heard answering that last bit of rubbish from the other end of the phone call. Bunny decided that he needed to step in to save the lovely girl from the imbecile.

'I don't think that a gentleman should be speaking with a lady in that tone, sir,' said Bunny to Milind, again loud enough for Tarana to hear. 'You should be polite and civil while getting your point across, especially with a sweet girl like Tarana. And, most especially, when it's her birthday!'

His boss's jaw fell. Milind Sathe was not used to being ticked off. His face turned a bright shade of red and he slammed the phone down.

'How dare you speak with me in that condescending tone, Kapoor!' said he to his deputy. 'I shall take up the matter of your misbehaviour with my Uncle, for sure!'

'Misbehaviour, sir? Are you sure you're not the one who's out-of-line at the moment?' was Bunny's rather bold retort.

There are times in the lives of men when words outlive their utility and the eyes say everything that is to be said. This was one such time. Both men glared at each other as if about to come to fisticuffs. Their eyes were locked in fierce combat. But, suddenly, Milind's face transformed itself into one that looked like that of a petulant three year old. Bunny knew that he had bitten off more than he could perhaps chew, and feared that he might lose his job, but he did not let that thought deter the fire that his eyes were directing towards the pesky-young-upstart that was his boss.

The following morning, Bunny walked about in the premises of Catalyst Multiplex more briskly than usual. It was not yet time for the gates to open, but there was much work to be done. He stopped in his tracks as he spied Tarana 'flowing' towards him with a smile on her lips. She was looking even more effervescent than she had during her birthday lunch. A gorgeous pink dress was making her look like a flower in full bloom. Bunny was in a hurry, but he smiled back and waited for her. How could he not?

'Bunny! How nice to see you first thing in the morning! I want to thank you for the gift and for the support yesterday,' she addressed him warmly, even affectionately.

'Also, I hear that the management has decided to attach me with you for implementing some new plans. That's great!' She smiled even more broadly at Bunny, and looked genuinely pleased at the prospect of working closely with him.

Bunny's heart was dancing to Tarana's words but he simply nodded and rushed to his cabin to ready himself for the day. There was much to be done! He was aware of the latest decisions of the management and, while he was thrilled at having Tarana work directly under him, he knew that he had only a month to prove himself. He paused to reflect upon the import of the previous night's phone call.

After his argument with Milind, Bunny had feared reprisal and admonishment at the hands of the Chairman. Wealthy uncles are not known to take lightly the fact that their beloved 'blue chip' nephews had been shown up by lowly managers.

Milind, as promised, had been missing from Tarana's birthday lunch, and Bunny had really enjoyed his absence. He'd also delighted in the fact that Tarana kept smiling at him all the while. They did not speak with each other much. But Bunny did not care. He knew that the scales had tilted. He had sensed that Tarana had taken a liking to him after his show of bravado during the exchange with Milind while she had been listening in.

After reaching his flat after an hour long journey (short by Mumbai standards), he had wondered how the management would view his 'insolence'.

The Chairman had called precisely at 9 pm.

'Good evening, sir,' was the greeting from Bunny, a tremor evident in his voice.

'Kapoor, you've been naughty today! I should fire you for your impetuosity, but I know that you're a bright chap, so I'm giving you one month to prove yourself. If you succeed in bringing in the crowds, you'll get a raise, or else you can go back home. Got the point, my boy?'

To say 'Yes, sir' was Bunny's only option; he opted for it.

'And, by the way, that pretty girl—what's her name?—will be working on your team from now on. I want results my boy, get it? Good night!' concluded the Chairman, without waiting for any further utterance from Bunny.

As he now glanced at the mirror once more to ready himself for the day ahead, he noticed that he looked good. His hair was neatly in place; his tie was nice and straight. His clean shaven face looked radiant. Bunny smiled at himself and turned to face the world.

He rushed to the ticket window and found to his satisfaction that there was already a queue. The latest blockbuster from Bollywood, *Bad luck,* had brought good luck back to Catalyst. It had hit the silver screen two days ago and was already doing healthy business. Bunny wondered why Hindi films had English titles these days but he was not complaining as long as the cash counters continued ringing. He made a mental note to instruct the youngster at the counter to improve his public-dealing skills. He wasn't quite satisfied with the impatient manner in which the lad was addressing a confused old lady.

The next few days passed in a whirl. Bunny woke up each morning to optimistic thoughts of crowded ticket windows. He fought every day against challenges posed by irritating customers (who wanted to meet the manager), by shirking subordinates (who did not realize the gravity of situations), by periods of self-doubt (when he saw seats empty in the halls), and by a distraction named Tarana (whenever she was in his vicinity, which was quite often).

It was particularly difficult for him to work in her presence. She would ask him for instructions frequently and he would have to advise her to the best of his ability, but the moment he would sense that she was being extra-warm, he would withdraw into his shell. She would walk away with a puzzled look on her pretty face, but Bunny knew that it was for the greater good. He had to think of the long run. He had to ensure that he and his team delivered results for his job to be safe and for Tarana to be his!

For the whole month, Bunny behaved like a tireless workaholic. When the big day came, he felt really fatigued but the smile on his face said it all. Catalyst Multiplex had never had it so good. Bunny's team had beaten all records hollow!

The Chairman of Catalyst Multiplexes Ltd, Ritesh Sathe, was a portly man with a pink face that often looked like it would burst. Thankfully, it never did. He now sat at the head of the table in the conference room at Catalyst, and as he addressed the staff seated before him, the man on his left looked like a beaten up movie-villain who was plotting revenge.

Milind Sathe had kept a low profile for the past 30 days, and had seldom been to office. He was miffed at the fact that his plea to sack Bunny had been turned down by his Uncle Ritesh. As he now sat listening to the senior Sathe, he occasionally glanced at the young lady seated next to him, and, on each such occasion, his face would display an even worse scowl than the one before. He avoided all form of contact with the man on the Chairman's right, our Bunny.

Bunny's smile was broadening by the second, as Ritesh Sathe spoke. The Chairman was not one to be miserly with praise when it was well earned. He showered one accolade after another.

'Team Catalyst, I'm so proud of you that I could hug you all! Bunny Kapoor, you have exceeded all expectations. Our cinemas have seen an occupancy rate of 90 per cent during the month, an occurrence that has never before been possible at Catalyst. Our shopping arcade has seen more footfalls than ever. I am delighted to inform you that we are now the number one multiplex in the whole of Mumbai!' announced the Chairman with pride, his pink face glowing.

Bunny beamed more and Milind scowled even more as the Chairman continued.

'I hereby announce a bonus of 20 per cent for all you lovely people,' declared the Chairman in a booming voice. 'And I hereby promote Bunny Kapoor to the post of Senior Manager, with an increment of 50 per cent in his monthly salary!'

Bunny and the staff were thrilled to bits! Tarana looked particularly delighted, and she stood up suddenly and whistled loudly, much to everyone's surprise, and much to the chagrin of the junior Sathe, who, as we have already learnt, was seated adjacent to her, and who had now closed his ears with his hands as if to protect his eardrums.

The Chairman appeared pleased at this exuberant response to his magnanimous pronouncements. He decided that this was an appropriate moment to make a grand exit. He got up to leave, and did so, but not before back-slapping Bunny while completely ignoring his nephew. The latter, whose face looked even worse than before, decided that it was time for him to make an exit too, and he stormed out after his uncle.

The conference room at Catalyst Multiplex erupted with joy, with everyone clapping and cheering unabashedly at the joyous news. Much back-slapping and hand-pumping went around. Bunny was backsplapped even by his juniors and more than everyone else, but he did not mind at all. He finally glanced at Tarana, who was still whistling intermittently and jumping up and down like a child.

Bunny Kapoor knew that he had won the day. He also knew that the enemy still had some venom left, and that further challenges awaited him in the days ahead. But he also knew that this was an occasion to celebrate, and that the timing was right.

'How about a date tonight?' he said to Tarana, who luckily heard the question over the general cacophony, probably because she had been waiting for it.

'I thought you'd never ask!' she said, and resumed her whistling and jumping.

Tarana walked even more majestically than usual as she neared Bunny's table and smiled at him as she did so.

'How many of those do you still have with you?' asked Bunny of her as she finally drew near.

'How many of what, Bunny?' was her quizzical response.

'Those thousand-watt smiles, Tarana. You can solve our country's power problems with them!' Bunny replied, his romantic charm at its peak. Tarana could only blush.

The venue for their first ever date was a chic new open-air coffee lounge that had recently opened in Bandra. The ambiance was cheery, the music was peppy and the evening air pleasant. There weren't too many other people around. It was the perfect setting.

'Tarana, well, I've been, er... how do you say, a little withdrawn over the past few weeks, but I must assure you that I've been very keen to date you,' said Bunny, once they were seated across each other.

'Well I guessed so, Mr. Kapoor!' replied Tarana, in her most musical voice. 'I hope I wasn't giving out too many signals that I was dying to go out with you!'

Bunny was not a man to blush easily, but Tarana was a stunner, and the manner in which the last sentence was uttered, along with its happy contents, made him do just that. For once, he was at a loss for words.

After a pause, which seemed a year-long to them, they spoke at once.

'I think I've fallen for you...' was Tarana's confession.

'I think I'm attracted to you...' was Bunny's.

Bunny's cheeks went darker red, and Tarana's turned that shade of pink that only the cheeks of the most beautiful girls do. She looked down at her hands. They were pretty too, noticed Bunny. He stretched out his own hand and touched one of them.

'Our cold coffee with ice-cream is delightful, madam and sir,' said a balding waiter, standing right next to their table, forcing Bunny to retreat. How typically a Bollywood-movie-like situation!

Bunny realized that he'd heard someone coughing during the course of the past few moments of magic, but he had not realised that he was the one whose attention the garcon had been trying to draw.

'Right sir, two cold coffees with ice-cream coming up!' said the man, without waiting for a response, since none seemed forthcoming from either of the two guests, so deep were they in the spell that young people often find themselves in. The balding waiter had evidently served many young couples in his time, and knew that it was best to draw his own conclusions on such occasions. Off he went to fetch the order.

Bunny and Tarana smiled at each other. In fact, they couldn't stop smiling, so happy were they to be alone with each other again.

'I've wanted to talk to you ever since you stood up to that brat, Milind Sathe. He's such a joker!' said Tarana, after another long pause. 'The manner in which you ticked him off was really impressive.'

'Well, he deserved it for being nasty to you,' said Bunny. 'But I must admit that it was a bit of gamble. I thought I'd be fired there and then!'

'Thank God you weren't! I was worried too. I've known Milind from our college days and he wasn't so bad then. Nowadays, he's quite unbearable and I've stopped talking to him altogether.'

'So have I!' said Bunny, and they burst out laughing at the memory of Milind seated at the conference table that morning, with the most pathetic of looks on his face.

'Watch out for him, though. He's a scheming guy and he won't take this setback lightly,' warned Tarana.

'I know. He'll be gunning for me, but I'm not the sort of chap to be easily put down,' Bunny said, not wanting to be modest before his new girlfriend.

'I know that, Bunny, and I also know that you kept avoiding me the whole of last month because you wanted to focus on the job at hand,' she said with a lopsided grin.

'Well, I must admit that you're quite a distraction and you would have slowed my work down considerably if we'd had this date last month!' he grinned back and held her hand once again.

'Here we are!' declared the balding gentleman, as he nonchalantly presented two large-sized glasses with delicious looking contents.

Bunny's hand retreated once again. He smiled at the man and thanked him.

'Enjoy your drink. Can I get you something else?' asked the man.

Tarana and Bunny had recovered sufficiently to respond this time. They shook their heads, and the garcon walked off with a smile on his face.

'He does have a perfect timing, doesn't he?' said Bunny, and they laughed again. Her soft angelic laugh blended well with his throaty one.

They took a sip each, looked deep into each other's eyes, and did not need to say much more that evening.

In the following weeks, Bunny and Tarana often met at their favourite café and were served by the balding gentleman each time. They grew quite fond of him. They also went for long walks and longer drives. Romance blossomed. At work, though, they were quite professional, having decided that their feelings for each other should not affect their output. The staff knew that the manager and his deputy were now man-and-girl, and they were happy for them.

Catalyst Multiplex continued to do really well and Bunny continued to impress the management, for he delivered results day after day, with great support from Tarana and the team.

This happy set of trends was interrupted, though, with

the return to town of Milind Sathe, who'd been holidaying in Greece and cooking up nefarious schemes.

One day, Ritesh Sathe was on a round of the multiplex, accompanied by his nephew whose face carried a smirk. They came across Bunny, who was in an animated conversation with a staff member in his cabin. The latter retreated to his duties on seeing the big boss approach.

'Bunny, why are you not implementing the rules properly?' was the opening query posed by the Chairman.

'In what regard, sir?' asked a puzzled Bunny.

'Why haven't you been marking your in-time and out-time in the designated register, and why hasn't Tarana been doing so either? I also hear that the two of you are quite cosy with each other at work nowadays.' The Chairman sounded stern as he divulged the reasons for his opening query.

Bunny glanced quickly at the smiling Milind, decided against punching him in the face and turned to the Chairman to rebut this personal attack.

'Sir, I do not think that my relationship with Tarana is a matter for you to comment on, especially since we do not let it affect our work,' Bunny's tone was pained yet defiant.

'Bunny, my boy, I have stood by you all this while and have been happy with your work, but contrary to your statement, Milind tells me that he has evidence to prove that you have disregarded the rules recently. You have spent many hours in recent weeks closeted in your cabin with the girl. I cannot allow such indiscipline at Catalyst. What would the staff think? Soon I'll have them all indulging in behaviour of this sort! I have as many girls working here as boys. I'm sure you know that, Mr. Manager!'

'May I see the evidence that he has, sir? It's a bunch of lies, I tell you!' Bunny was not going to give in without a fight here!

'I do not have to show you any evidence, Bunny. All I will say is that this is your last warning, and you'd better watch out!' The senior Sathe banged a fist on the wooden railing as he ended the conversation with these emphatic words, his face on the verge of exploding. Realizing that he had overdone the bang, he winced with pain and walked away.

Bunny clenched his own fist, and Milind pumped the air with his. Bunny looked Milind in the eye once more, and almost burnt him alive with the fire emanating from his.

'You'd better be at your best behaviour, Kapoor! Do not add insubordination to the growing list of your transgressions.' Milind's evil grin set Bunny's blood boiling.

He walked out with the air of one making a successful comeback, and almost bumped into the incoming Tarana at the exit. She turned and glared at him. Milind did not seem to notice and left the scene.

'What's happening here, Bunny? That rogue had a smirk on his face and you have a frown on yours,' remarked the observant lass to her beau.

'Milind has been making false allegations about you and me getting cosy in my cabin instead of working,' explained Bunny, as Tarana's face went very pink.

'The scoundrel! I'll teach him a lesson he'll never forget,' she declared in a voice that was unlike her normally melodious one.

She had just held Bunny's hand to console him when in walked Milind again. Tarana and he were always being interrupted when they held hands, rued Bunny. But he realized that it was not the time to ponder over trivialities. There were more pressing matters at hand!

'Aha!' exclaimed the intruder, as Tarana's hand withdrew abruptly to its normal position at her side. 'I see that you haven't learnt your lesson and are still engaging in physical activities here. I will go and report this right away!' Milind turned to leave once more.

'Just a moment, you rat!' Tarana's voice had grown even fiercer since it had last been used. She took two quick steps, caught up with Milind, and tapped him firmly on the shoulder, forcing him to turn.

There are some sounds that appeal more to certain people than to others. The sound of a woman's hand on a man's cheek is one such sound. The extent or absence of the appeal of this sound depends not only upon the force with which the said hand touches the face in question, but also upon whether one is the recipient or just an onlooker. From the loudness of the sound he heard then, Bunny knew that Tarana had slapped Milind really hard!

Bunny, the onlooker, felt proud of his woman, and Milind, the recipient, did not feel good at all. Tarana, on her part, was still on the attack, and was readying herself for another assault.

'How dare you spread lies about Bunny and me?' she addressed Milind in a shrill, threatening tone, with her right arm raised to strike Milind on his left cheek once more.

'I shall have you arrested for this!' was all that Milind could say before the second slap was heard, this time loud enough for people in the foyer outside to turn and gape through the glass wall of Bunny's cabin.

Bunny wanted to hit Milind himself. But he knew that Tarana had better be stopped before the situation got out of hand!

He took Tarana's hand and pulled her towards himself. Milind Sathe made a more pathetic face than he had ever done, mumbled something about calling the police and rushed out to complain once more to uncle dearest.

Bunny Kapoor, Manager of Catalyst Multiplex, Juhu, Mumbai, knew that he and his deputy had better start looking for new jobs soon, for this might be the end of their tryst at Catalyst.

He wiped what looked like a tear from Tarana's face. She was obviously hurt by the false allegations that Milind had levied upon them. Bunny realised that she was fonder of him than any girl had been till date.

The way in which she looked at him now, as they stood face to face, hand in hand, reflected a set of feelings that were nothing short of deep attachment. Bunny felt touched but he also felt slightly uncomfortable.

'Am I ready for such an attachment?' he asked himself.

He turned and noticed that some staff members were gathered near his window, and were peering in to make sense of the commotion that had very recently occurred in his cabin. With a wave of a hand, Bunny shooed them off and they scurried away. That done, he addressed the lovely Tarana, one of whose hands was still miraculously in one of his, uninterruptedly so. She was beginning to sob.

'Tarana, take control of your emotions,' he began. 'There was no point losing your temper like that. We have probably just lost our jobs as a result!'

The effect of his words upon Tarana was such that the floodgates of her eyes opened. The brave girl, who had twice slapped the nephew of the big boss just a while back, now began to weep openly and, some seconds later, even began to howl. So sudden was her outburst and so loud was the sound of her wailing that the same group that had recently been shooed away returned to gape through the window once more to check out the latest.

Tarana kept crying like a baby who had broken her favourite toy and did not know whom to blame for it. Despite Bunny's reassuring tone and words, she just did not stop. Bunny was not sure what to do.

'Tarana, come on! You're a big girl, and you showed some real guts out there. You cannot let yourself down now by howling like this,' he said to her.

'But, but....How will we ever work together again, Bunny? I just love working here with you. That rogue has ruined everything!' Tarana said amid loud wails and streams of tears.

Bunny knew that he had to act. Pronto!

Twenty minutes later, Tarana and he were in the Chairman's office standing before a massive desk and facing the large occupant of the chair behind it. At one side of the gigantic table, the familiarly loathsome figure of Milind Sathe stood staring downward.

The senior Mr. Sathe was addressing the three of them.

'I must say that you have all behaved like errant children. Milind, I have learnt from reliable sources that your complaints about these two youngsters not marking their attendance and getting cosy in the cabin were totally false! You made me say scandalous and venomous things against innocent young people!'

Milind continued to look as if he had been admonished by his class teacher. Tarana turned to glare at him. Bunny smiled as he continued to look at the Chairman.

'However, slapping a senior official of the organization and creating a ruckus in office is an unpardonable offence, and this young lady will have to pay for it!' continued the big boss.

'Sir, if I may speak for a minute,' requested Bunny. 'False allegations against any young lady are bound to distress her no end. Your nephew is responsible for this unpleasant situation and he must apologize to the two of us.'

Tarana nodded in agreement and Milind turned to see his uncle's reaction to this request. The uncle-nephew relationship was clearly facing a severe test here. Ritesh Sathe sighed.

It has already been pointed out that the senior Sathe was a large hearted man. He clearly wanted to end this unpleasantness there and then.

'Yes Milind, you must apologise to Bunny and Tarana! I want this to be the end of animosity between you and these two, do you hear? And as for the slapping bit, we shall pardon the young lady this time, but shall take from her a written commitment that such violence shall not be repeated ever again by her,' the senior Sathe announced.

Milind knew that he had been defeated yet again. He mumbled an apology and walked out sheepishly, this time with a resigned look on his face.

The Chairman opened his mouth to speak again, but Bunny interjected.

'I must thank you, sir, for your just and judicious approach. However, I must submit my resignation here and now, for I cannot work anymore under such circumstances,' he said, as two jaws fell in the room, one a little more than the other.

'Why, Bunny?' was the question from both Tarana and the Chairman. Their tones were similarly incredulous.

'I have decided to move on. Catalyst is now in the forefront of all multiplexes in the city of Mumbai, thanks to you, Tarana, and to you Mr Chairman. Without your support, I could not have achieved all this…' Bunny continued.

'Now, with no real challenge confronting me work-wise, and with your nephew hating my guts, Mr. Sathe, I feel it would be best for me to make an exit. I do not want to be the cause of such antagonism here anymore,' he concluded.

Ritesh Sathe's jaw regained its normal position, for he saw logic in Bunny's assertions. Tarana's did too, but her face was red, and her eyes were wet. Another outburst was coming, for sure.

'How dare you, Bunny! You cannot decide these things unilaterally! What about my feelings? How can you leave like this?' she said, with a piercing look and with tears beginning to roll down her red cheeks.

'Tarana! I never said I'm leaving you!' said Bunny. 'I merely want to work elsewhere in the city. We shall continue to meet every day!' He held her hands, both of them, to reassure her.

Tarana's face regained some of its original light pink, and the tears stopped mid-way on her cheeks. She even managed a smile.

'Oh, Bunny! I think you're right. You're so right!' she flung herself into his arms with these words.

The Chairman got up with a loud 'Ahem', and Milind, as was his wont, walked into the room at that very instant.

Bunny was in no mood for retreating though, and he held his girl tight.

He had stood his ground, he had won the war, and he had Tarana in his arms. The Chairman's nephew could go fly a kite for all he cared. He was no longer Bunny's boss.

Bunny sighed as he settled deep into his bean bag a few weeks later. He had returned from Goa after a longish holiday and had spent many hours by the sea, thinking about life as a whole.

He knew that Tarana and he were as compatible as any young couple could be, but he also knew that he wasn't ready yet to take the plunge and get married. He had discussed this with Tarana and she had understood. In fact, she was planning to do a post-graduate degree from an American university and was soon going to be on a flight. They had decided to part as friends and keep in touch but without any commitment.

Mumbai would not be the same without her. It was time for him to move on, again.

3

Banking On Bunny!

Bunny was completely unsure of himself in the banking world and had thus appeared for the interview with considerable trepidation. The lady in the chair was intimidating but also attractive. She glared at him over her glasses.

'Mr. Kapoor! You know nothing about banking. Why have you applied for this job?' she demanded of him.

'Ma'am!' he blurted out, worried that the interview might soon be over. 'I know a thing or two about coaxing people into listening to me, and I'm sure I can be a successful marketing professional. Why don't you try me out? I'm certain that I can open a large number of accounts for you within a week!'

Bunny realised as he uttered these words that he'd bitten off more than he could chew. He knew nothing about opening accounts. The intimidating lady gave him another glare. He was seeing visions of her calling in the security to throw him out when her face transformed itself into a smiling one. 'She is looking quite resplendent now,' thought Bunny. 'Her green sari's suiting her well.'

'I'm not the sort to fall for such tactics, Mr. Kapoor. I've seen many imposters in my time, and while I am not saying that you are one, I am not convinced by your bravado. However...'

She paused at this point and smiled even more broadly at him. Her teeth were very white and perfectly formed, noticed Bunny, except one which was yellowish.

It is no secret that in the history of the world the word 'however' has been used millions of times. However, it has never carried as much hope for any human being as it did for Bunny Kapoor at that moment.

He looked at her mouth carefully, waiting breathlessly for some good news to emanate from it. After what seemed like an eternity, she finally resumed speaking.

'...there's a spark in your eye that I like. I'm, therefore, willing to give you fifteen days to open fifteen accounts. If you do so, you're hired!'

Bunny looked at her open-mouthed and decided to search in his mirror later for the mysterious spark in his eye that seemed to impress the female-folk so much. There were more pressing matters to be tackled at that moment, however.

'Done, Ma'am, I shall give it my all and I assure you that I won't let you down!' Bunny smiled back at her and accepted her offer enthusiastically.

He got up and shook hands with her. She looked at him kindly.

'Don't plunge headlong into something that you cannot handle, Mr. Kapoor. Plan and prepare!' was her advice as she turned to leave the room.

By the time Bunny nodded, she was already half way down the corridor. He was even more impressed. Quite a woman!

Turning towards an insignificant other in the room, Bunny enquired about the interviewer's name.

'Mrs. Chari,' was the response he got and for the time being that satisfied him.

She looked every bit as if her name should indeed be Mrs. Chari. A first name was not relevant at that juncture.

He took a few deep breaths and made his own way out of the hall. He had no time to lose.

Bunny spent three precious days sitting with a bespectacled gentleman known only as Shankar. He wasn't given any offer letter or formal communication. He knew that Mrs. Chari's offer was purely her own decision and that he'd better make the most of it if he wanted to land the job.

Bunny focused on whatever he needed to know for opening accounts, without trying to learn the non-essentials. Shankar was an excellent trainer and Bunny a sharp cookie. They hit it off well. At the end of Day 3, Shankar extended a hand and Bunny shook it vigorously.

'You're a good learner, Bunny. Go ahead and make a mark!' Shankar said, encouragingly.

Bunny thanked him profusely and prayed that he indeed proved to be a hit in this new world.

He'd slept well, woken up early and set off sporting a tie (along with a shirt and trousers). He carried a briefcase, looked totally like a marketing chap, and felt like one too. Bunny's first stop was a school. He'd made some enquiries about the sort of targets he should aim for, and had been told that middle-aged teachers were a good option. He wrote out his name on a slip of paper and the peon took it inside to the

Principal, whose name evidently was Lekha Chandran (the name plate said so).

On being summoned, Bunny soon found himself face to face with the target herself. He sat down on being motioned to do so and sized up his first potential customer.

Bunny had not bargained for the fact that middle-aged ladies could also be so formidable in appearance and presence. This one clearly weighed over a hundred kilos. The chair beneath her was not visible but Bunny was sure that it was made of the hardest material known to mankind. It was, after all, still intact.

'What can I do for you, Mr. B. Kapoor?' was her question.

She had a voice to match. 'Booming' is the only word to describe it. She eyed him through her oddly tiny, round glasses as Bunny squirmed in his seat.

'Well, B. Kapoor?' she thundered, dropping the 'Mr.' and all related formalities. 'I don't have all day, you know!'

'Mrs. Chandran, I'm here to open your account with Vera Bank, the finest bank in the world.' Bunny was quite satisfied with his opening statement.

The weighty target leant forward till she was within arm's length of him. She gave him a really fierce look, forcing Bunny to lean as far back as possible in his chair.

'Kapoor, for your information, I'm not married, so you can't address me as "Mrs." What's more, my name is not Lekha Chandran! The name plate outside was my predecessor's and she left a week ago. I have not had time to get it changed. Now will you buzz off, or should I help you out personally?' Her voice was so loud that it could probably be heard by Mrs. Chari in her office miles away.

'Thank you, ma'am, whatever your name is!' said Bunny as he fled from her, afraid that she might carry out her threat of helping him out 'personally'. His 70 kilos would not be much for her to lift up and throw out, he guessed.

'Ouch!' he thought to himself, as he left the premises of the school.

He'd come quite close to becoming a target himself.

Feeling disheartened, he sat in an old coffee shop for a while and sipped away. He didn't even notice the searing heat. He was much too engrossed in thought.

Bunny wondered if he'd done the right thing by shifting to Chennai. The city was new to him and so was the kind of job he was trying to get into.

He figured that no Herculean effort would help to make a success of this one. He was about to get up and make his way back to the bank to inform Mrs. Chari that he had failed miserably when he heard a woman singing.

He turned to find a pleasant looking lady, clad in an expensive sari, sipping coffee at the rather ramshackle coffee stall and singing to herself intermittently. She smiled at him and enquired whether he was a marketing professional.

He looked down at his tie and smiled.

'Indeed I am, Ma'am. Can I join you for a bit?' he requested.

On receiving a nod, he went up to her table and sat on a smallish chair.

'You look a bit downcast. Is all not going as it should?' she asked him.

He blushed at being sized up so easily by a stranger.

'You're spot on, ma'am! I'm trying to get some new accounts for a bank and my first encounter was a disaster!' Bunny confessed without hesitation.

She smiled at him again, as women often did. He wanted to ask what she was doing at a shabby coffee stall when she could probably afford a much better setting for her mid-morning outing. She read his thoughts again.

'You're wondering why I'm sitting here sipping coffee. Well, this place is full of memories for me. I come here once every week. And I love to sing, so that's what I'm doing.'

'Why don't you sing some more, ma'am? You have a wonderful voice!' Bunny had taken an instant liking to this genteel woman.

'Sure!' she said, and needed no second invitation. She sang melodiously and full-throatedly. The words were alien to him but he enjoyed listening to her. Some people gathered around. The coffee-stall owner, a kindly old man, smiled. He was probably used to this.

When she ended her mellifluous song, there was a hearty round of applause and she took a bow. Everyone then went back to their own business.

'You are a very accomplished singer!' said Bunny.

She addressed him softly, her voice still in the musical mode.

'Why don't you open an account for me? I can start with a couple of lacs of rupees. Would that be fine?'

Though Bunny Kapoor was used to surprises, there were some which made his heart sing, his goose pimples rise and mouth quiver. This was surely one such.

'Really, ma'am? You can't be serious! You don't even know me and you haven't heard about our schemes yet as well.'

'My name is Sreedhara. Do not call me 'ma'am'! Now forget the formalities. Go ahead and open my account. I don't have much time!'

Bunny didn't know how to react. What a stroke of luck! And to think that he'd been all set to throw in the towel.

He pulled out the requisite forms and filled them up eagerly, with inputs from her. Five minutes later, he had obtained her signatures and opened his first account.

Bunny Kapoor was not a demonstrative man, but he felt compelled to stand up on his chair at this magnificent development and whistle loudly. He did just that.

The coffee-stall owner smiled at him. Perhaps he had people singing and whistling in his café every day, for he did not seem surprised at all. Sreedhara gave Bunny another pleasant smile.

'I can see how much that meant to you, my boy. I'm delighted to be able to help. Should I give you a few references too?'

'I'm really grateful, ma'am! And how did you guess that I was going to ask you for references? You really are quite a mind-reader!' Bunny gushed.

'Would you stop calling me 'ma'am'? It makes me feel old. Now here are the contact numbers. They're all friends, so just call them up and go meet them with my reference.' She browsed through the list of contacts in her mobile phone and made him write down a dozen names and numbers.

As they sipped some more coffee, he told her a bit more about himself, of the intimidating Mrs. Chari, of her challenge to him, and of his ever-increasing urge to succeed in each endeavour, including this one.

'Are you my guardian angel? I'm so lucky to have met you!' Bunny thanked his new found friend.

'See you next Thursday, young man, same place, same time. And you'll have to treat me to coffee!' Sreedhara got up abruptly, and walked out hurriedly.

Bunny was not complaining. He was thrilled to bits. Now he could get cracking at those references and open more accounts. It was the only thing that he wanted to do at the time.

A week later, Bunny's score was six. He still had nine more accounts to open, and only a few days left to do so. He knew that Mrs. Chari would give him no further extension.

Five of Sreedhara's friends, all married women, had agreed to open their accounts. What's more, he was fed very generously when he had visited them. He got to eat loads of *idlis* with piping hot *sambhar* and had loved them. Moving to Chennai was not such a bad idea after all!

Sreedhara's friends had been very warm and friendly. Bunny realized that she was a very popular woman and he wanted to know more about her. And, so, he arrived well before the designated hour the next Thursday. Sreedhara was there already! He treaded softly and sat on a chair behind her. She was singing in full flow and the audience seemed enthralled. Some twenty men and women from nearby shops had assembled to listen.

She was dressed even more elaborately than the last time and looked very much out of place, but obviously felt at home. Again the applause was deafening and she loved it.

Bunny now went and sat opposite her.

'Oh!' she exclaimed. 'When did you arrive?'

'Just a little while ago. I was enjoying your song. Have you ever performed on stage?' he enquired.

'Yes, I have. In fact, I still do. But nothing quite gives me the same high as singing at this coffee stall. It brings back memories of the time when I was just a beginner and used to sit here and sing. Two decades back!' she explained.

'Oh!' it was his turn to be surprised. 'So you're a professional singer and you come here for old times' sake. I'm impressed!'

'Oh, come on! Don't embarrass me now. How's your marketing doing? And aren't you going to order me some coffee like you'd promised?' she smiled her winsome smile yet again.

Bunny grinned and signalled to the gentle old man accordingly. He then turned to his benefactress to update her.

'I'm still short of half way there, Sreedhara! Some of your friends agreed, some didn't. I need your advice on how to finish the task.'

'Not to worry! I'm not in a hurry today. Let's invite some people here and open their accounts on the spot! Do you have enough forms?' she asked him, quite casually.

Bunny took a deep breath and nodded. He actually had a lump in his throat, something he was not used to. This woman was really unbelievable. God surely had something to do with her entry into his life.

Sreedhara was on the phone already. She called up one friend after another, gave the willing ones different time slots and the address, and sure enough, the first of the gullible targets walked into thc coffee stall twenty minutes later.

Sreedhara winked at Bunny. She then proceeded to give the thin studious looking entrant a hug and ordered coffee for the three of them. She really loved coffee, this angel from the heavens.

The thin lady was in a hurry and was done with her coffee and with the opening of her account within ten minutes. As simple as that!

The next one was a tough customer. She arrived on time,

but seemed to have an old grouse with Sreedhara's family and would not stop talking about it. Bunny was not used to being ignored by women, but this one behaved as if he did not exist.

'Sree, I wanted to meet you personally to complain about your brother's behaviour. I must tell you that he was most rude to me at your last performance and I'm not one to forget such misdemeanour in a hurry. He must apologise to me personally or I'll go to town with the story of his insolence! He ignored me completely and did not even smile when he crossed me.'

The tough customer, thus, adopted an unflinching attitude.

Sreedhara had been grinning all this while, and had even directed a quick wink in the direction of Bunny, who was still smarting at not being noticed.

Sreedhara waited for her friend to calm down before finally speaking.

'Malti, I'll scold him personally for behaving so badly. How dare he! Now tell me, would you like to open an account with this young man's bank?'

The effect of this statement was quite dramatic. Malti looked satisfied at Sreedhara's assurance and turned to size up the male presence at the table. Her expression changed from the antagonistic to the gentle. She checked to see if her hair was in place and smiled at Bunny.

'Oh, Sree! I didn't notice this cute young boy sitting here all this while, so involved was I in giving vent to my feelings. How handsome he is, don't you think?'

Sreedhara nodded. Bunny turned pink. He recalled his days as a toddler, when two aunties would gang up on him to his utter discomfort and declare him very cute. Thankfully, this time the two ladies did not pinch his cheek as the aunties used to.

Not noticing that the other two were rather quiet in her presence, Malti continued with her monologue.

'Come, come, young man, I haven't got all day! Get those nice looking hands to fill up my form for me. I can't refuse Sree anything, and besides, you're far too handsome to say 'no' to.'

Bunny looked at his hands and then glanced at Sreedhara. They grinned at each other and Bunny got down to filling up another form.

Once he had received the tough customer's cheque and a host of additional compliments, Bunny relaxed.

'Seven more to go!' he thought to himself.

Malti got up, gave each of them a peck on the cheek and scurried away with the air of one who had accomplished all her life's goals.

Sreedhara gave Bunny a motherly look and sympathized with him.

'My apologies, Bunny! I hate having to put you through all this, but then some of my friends are a bit crazy. Malti, of course, takes the cake!'

Bunny disagreed. In fact, he needed more targets like Malti.

'Sreedhara, without you I would not have been able to make a start in this city. I'm totally beholden to you. There are no words with which I can express my gratitude to you for what you've done...'

'Bunny, Bunny! I'm going to walk away if you embarrass me any further.'

She held his hand.

'Just don't think about it anymore. You're like a younger brother. My brother, Rajan, is about your age, and is just as handsome. That's why our friend Malti didn't like the fact that he ignored her! Would I not have done all this for him too? Now shut up and just keep filling up forms. Here comes the next account!'

For the next few hours, Bunny did not open his mouth except to order more coffee. Sreedhara's friends walked in and out of the little coffee stall and signed on the dotted line with minimum fuss. By four o'clock, he had achieved the mother of all targets! Fifteen accounts were in the bag, and he still had a few days left. Mrs. Chari would be delighted, he was sure, and he would be appointed on a regular basis. All thanks to Sreedhara.

The two of them walked out together. He made her agree that she would accept a dinner invitation from him at any place other than the coffee-stall.

'Certainly, Bunny. First settle into your job, and get your first pay cheque. Then I'll go out for dinner with you.'

'Will you sing too?'

'Of course, I will! I'll sing in English and Hindi for you. Now run along and meet that fearsome boss of yours to give her the good news. But remember to not mention to anyone in your bank that I helped you. I don't want them pestering me for more business!'

She walked away to a swanky looking car. A chauffer in uniform opened the door for her, she got inside and the car zipped away.

Bunny paid the genteel coffee stall owner a hundred rupees for the unending supply of beverages, hailed an auto and made his way to the bank.

Mrs. Chari stared at him as he walked into her room on being permitted to do so. She was wearing a pleasant looking pink sari that gave her a very cheerful look, but her eyes were still fiery.

'Well? How did you do? Don't you still have a few days to go?' she wasted no time in getting down to the point.

He pulled out a list and handed it over. She looked at it rather disbelievingly.

'I've handed over the forms to Shankar and he's processing them,' Bunny informed the boss.

Mrs. Chari's expression changed several times as she went through the list of accounts opened by Bunny. He watched her closely. She finally looked up.

'Why are you staring at me, Mr. Kapoor? I don't like men eyeing me like that! I'm impressed with your work though, and with your list. Some of these ladies are well known names, and they should be good clients for us. Some day you'll have to make a presentation to the team on how you managed to get your first 15 accounts. But tell me, how is it that all of them are women?' she gave him a disapproving look as she uttered the last sentence.

'Ma'am, I got really lucky!' was all that he could blurt out.

Blurting out short sentences was his only option in his boss's presence. He wondered, though, why she'd felt uncomfortable at his gaze. He also wondered why she'd disapproved of the fact that all his accounts were female ones.

'Whatever!' she said before picking up her phone and telling someone at the other end to issue him an appointment letter.

'Welcome aboard, Mr. Kapoor!' She shook hands with him

and flashed him the dazzling smile, which he remembered well from the day of the interview. One of her teeth was still yellowish. Bunny also noted that her hand was cold, perhaps an indication that she was a cold-blooded human being. But something about her was endearing too.

'I knew that the spark in your eye should be given a chance. Your target will remain one account per day. Mr. Madhavan will give you all the other details. All the best!'

She waved him away with these words.

Bunny was thrilled to have entered the big bad world of banking. He knew that he could be a winner here. He also knew that he could not depend solely on Sreedhara for achieving his targets. He had to find his own way of bagging them. Before going to Mr. Madhavan's cabin, Bunny made his way to the washroom and peered into the mirror to look for that fabled spark in his eye. He couldn't spot anything that looked like a spark, but if Mrs. Chari had said so, as had many others before her, it must exist. Perhaps only the ladies could spot it!

He grinned at himself, pumped his fist, and made his way away from the washroom mirror and into Mr. Madhavan's cabin.

'Here you are, Mr. Kapoor. All the papers you'll need, including your appointment letter,' Mr. Madhavan said to him as he handed over some documents.

'Is that it, sir?' asked Bunny of him.

'Indeed! All the best, Mr. Kapoor.'

Mr. Madhavan shook his hand before shifting his attention to the huge pile of papers on his desk and Bunny realized immediately that he was one of those efficient people without whom no organization can run successfully.

Having thanked him, Bunny went straight to Shankar, who gave him a pat on the back.

'Well done, boy! You're the first one to be appointed here without any previous banking experience. You clearly have that something 'extra' in you, which would make you surge ahead of the pack. Go out there and get them!'

Bunny thanked him. With so much encouragement coming his way, Bunny had every reason to do well. Shankar was a great guy, and it was to him that Bunny would turn for advice in the months to come. He was determined to open at least ten accounts through his own efforts before meeting Sreedhara again. There was quite a bit of planning and execution to be done. Bunny Kapoor, newly appointed bank executive, was on the prowl!

Bunny entered the office of the Vice-President of a company in the Perambur area of Chennai with his heart beating fast. He had to prove Mrs. Chari wrong again by opening some 'male' accounts. He was a bit uncomfortable at her insinuation that he was good at opening only female ones.

The gentleman behind the huge desk looked cheerful and he gave him a warm handshake. Bunny wiped his neck with his handkerchief. Chennai's humidity is not easy to handle.

'One glass of water for the gentleman!' ordered his first male target on noticing that Bunny was hot and thirsty.

'Thank you, sir!' said Bunny, gulping down the contents of the glass that was brought to him.

'What can I do for you, Mr. Kapoor?' asked the Vice-President of him as he looked closely at Bunny's newly-printed business card.

'Well sir, I'm here to present before you the exciting options that our bank has brought out just for salaried persons like you. Can I tell you about them in some detail?' Bunny enquired.

'Ah! You're just the man I've been looking for!' said the gentleman behind the desk as he summoned a girl who had been reading a book in another part of the largish room.

'Preeti, meet Mr. Kapoor. He will open an account for you in Vera Bank.'

Bunny noticed her for the first time. She was tall and pretty, perhaps a college student. She was dressed in a contemporary looking pair of jeans and top. Smart and confident, she shook his hand firmly on approaching.

Bunny was keen to open the girl's account, but wondered whether the male of the species would elude him again.

'Sir, wouldn't you too like to open an account with us?' he enquired of the VP, a little hesitantly.

Preeti, meanwhile, was giving him wistful looks and staring at him in a rather forthright manner.

'Are you married, Mr. Kapoor?' the VP asked him, quite out of the blue.

Bunny shook his head truthfully, but wondered what he was getting into.

'We're looking for a match for Preeti. Is yours a permanent job with the Bank?' the VP continued with the interrogation.

Bunny glanced at Preeti for a split second, and wished that he hadn't. She was literally drooling over him by now. In front of her father!

'No, sir. I'm on probation for three months and I don't know whether I'll be confirmed. Moreover, if you're implying that I marry your daughter, I would beg to be excused, for I'm not into the marrying mode yet. Shall I fill up the form for your daughter?' Bunny decided to thus put the facts on the table.

The VP's face underwent a few mutations in the next few seconds, and reflected feelings of hope, despair, and disgust, in that order. His ears were emitting a smoke-like gas by now, and he got up with a start. His daughter stood up too, so Bunny decided to join them in that position, not wanting to be accused of bad manners.

'Please leave! You have rejected my beautiful daughter! How dare you?' the VP was fuming.

Bunny had perfected the art of wrapping up his stuff and leaving the scene in a hurry when a potential target became violent in intent. He was out of the room before the VP could say, 'I'll make sure that you lose your job!'

Bunny held his head with both hands as he awaited his lunch *thali* at a busy café in Egmore that afternoon. He was amazed at the gall of some people. Imagine being asked to marry someone in lieu of opening an account! How preposterous was that! It seemed the world was full of nutty jobs and nuttier people!

He must think of a new strategy.

His *thali* arrived and he dug into it for he loved Tamil cuisine. Accounts or no accounts, he would always remember his stint at Chennai for its piping hot *sambhar* as well as for Mrs. Chari and Sreedhara.

An elderly looking gentleman wanted to sit at his table and, as always, Bunny acquiesced readily.

Not much in the mood to speak, occupied as he was with thoughts of accounts and targets, Bunny munched his food without paying attention to the man.

'Aren't you the one who met our Principal the other day?' the man asked him.

Bunny's reverie broken, he realized that the query was directed at him. He turned to find the man looking vaguely familiar.

'Are you the one who ushered me into that fiery Principal's office? The office which had the name plate of Mrs. Chandran affixed outside?' asked Bunny of him.

'Yes, sir!' was the man's cheerful response. 'Now we've replaced the old name plate with one sporting Ms. Shetty's name.'

'So that's her name! I won't die wondering now! How do you work with her? I wonder why she hasn't eaten you up yet as if you were a *dosa*!'

The man laughed at Bunny's sense of humour, not realizing that he was half serious.

'I know what you mean, sir! But she's not that bad. Actually you annoyed her by calling her Mrs. Chandran!' the man explained.

'So, were you listening in?' asked Bunny with a smile.' What's your name?'

'My name's Ramanathan. Yes, sir, I was! Actually it's a good idea to keep tabs on a new Principal to find out about her ways; don't you think?'

Bunny nodded in agreement, though he wasn't convinced. Ramanathan continued to divulge more details.

'You know what, sir, she felt bad later at having shooed you away. She said so to me the next day. Why don't you meet her again to try and win her over?'

Bunny almost choked over an *uttapam*.

'Are you mad? She'll kill me this time!' he said on recovering sufficiently.

'No, sir! You're mistaken. She would not. Want to bet?' offered Ramanathan with a smile.

Bunny looked at Ramanathan in new light. The man obviously possessed superior qualities that were not easily discernible at first sight. Bunny realised that there were hitherto un-thought of possibilities here.

'Bet? No, Ramanathan, I'm not a 'betting' man. But I have a proposition for you: if you get her signatures on this form here, I'll give you a commission of a hundred rupees,' Bunny put his cards on the table thus.

'Done, sir! What if I get you more accounts? No teacher in the school would say no to me!' Ramanathan stood up as he made this offer, all excited about it.

Bunny could no longer sit either! He promised Ramanathan a hundred rupees for each account, and handed over ten forms to the man with some basic instructions. He could always call up the new account-holders to fill in the missing details later, he figured.

Ramanathan looked as if he couldn't wait to get back to school. He was off in a flash, leaving an untouched glass of butter-milk, which Bunny polished off in quick time.

He wondered if this new strategy would work. What he did not realize then was that he was going to have the answer in a matter of hours.

'Sir! Eight accounts already opened for you! Mrs. Shetty's is one of them. Would cash do instead of a cheque in some cases?' Ramanathan was speaking hysterically over the phone. Bunny listened to him with glee as he sat at his desk in the strongly air-conditioned premises of Vera Bank. No wonder Mrs. Chari's hands were so cold, thought Bunny.

But this was a moment to rejoice, he realized. Ramanathan was a goldmine. He had eight accounts in the bag in a single day! Mrs. Chari would be delighted, he knew.

'Ramanathan, that is excellent work. Yes, cash will do. Now tell me how many males and how many females are there on the list?' Bunny enquired.

'Males, sir? We don't have any males other than me in the whole school! It's a girls' school, you know! But I can get you another ten to twenty accounts for sure in the coming days.'

On the whole, Bunny was ecstatic at this information but he was wary of being the target of yet another barb from the boss when she'd see that there were still no males on his list.

'Oh, Ramanathan! Is it possible for you to open your own account with our bank too?' he enquired hopefully.

But Ramanathan had disconnected the phone by then. The male account would have to wait a little longer.

In the following weeks, Bunny became the star performer of Vera Bank, Chennai. He brought in customers quicker than anyone in the history of the bank.

Sreedhara and Ramanathan, an odd combination, managed to bring him more customers than he needed, in their own independent ways. It was only his personal pride that made him try to open accounts on his own too, with mixed results. Mrs. Chari had surely grown fond of him, though she scarcely showed it. She still glared at him at times and constantly pulled his leg for not having any males on his lists. Bunny had almost given up on men. On young women, too, for they were prone to falling for him. Thus, he focused only on forty-something women and their accounts.

His colleagues, including Shankar, started calling him

C-MAW, the Champion of Middle Aged Women but Bunny didn't mind at all. His salary and bonuses were enough to keep him comfortable, and he liked the work too. He was about to master another vertical in life, and he loved that fact. He loved Chennai too. The city had a calm but professional approach to life and work. People were, by and large, warm and friendly. And, of course, the food was a major attraction.

He seldom had occasion to meet Mrs. Chari, but one day she sent for him and he felt his heart skip a beat. She was a human being who demanded that one be sharp, alert, and on the ball all the time. She was on the phone when he entered her room. She waved to him to sit down (always a good sign, for she could also keep visitors standing). She was evidently discussing a serious matter with someone very senior. He watched her intermittently, not wanting to be accused of staring. She was dressed in a sheer blue sari and looked particularly vibrant. Her hair looked a bit different and suited her well. She looked more attractive than ever.

Mrs. Chari finally put down the phone. She wore a grave expression. It was after a whole minute that she spoke to him.

'Bunny, I've been addressing you as Mr. Kapoor for far too long,' she said, finally.

He looked at her and then looked at the wall, as girls sometimes do. For some reason, he felt shy and uncomfortable. She smiled warmly at him.

'Come on, Bunny. Don't tell me that you're nervous. I know that I scare people at times, but you've known me long enough. Now listen to me carefully.'

Bunny went red in the face at being found out, but leant forward a bit to be sure to catch her every word.

'There is a customer who has the potential to put our bank into serious trouble. She is upset about a recent incident and is threatening to go to the press with all kinds of stories. The Chairman was on the phone just now, and he wants me to nip the impending crisis in the bud,' she continued.

Bunny smiled, for he was quick on the uptake. She obviously wanted him to go and mollify the lady.

'I see that you've caught on, Bunny. Yes, I want you to go and meet her and dissuade her from babbling to the media. She's a tough woman and it won't be easy but I think you'll be able to do it.'

She leaned forward and looked him in the eye as she said the next words.

'Use your charm with her, Mr. Kapoor.'

Bunny did not flinch this time, and returned the look. Mrs. Chari was the one who was forced to look away. She mumbled something about the need for him to get the details from Shankar. He left wondering whether she was attracted to him.

Bunny rang the bell gingerly, hoping for the best but prepared for the worst. It was answered by a grim looking woman dressed in a night gown.

'Are you Mrs. Badrinath?' Bunny enquired, a little hesitantly.

'Your name?' was the counter question. The grim looking lady had a manly voice which went well with her dry exterior.

'Bunny Kapoor, from Vera Bank,' said Bunny, trying to hide his annoyance at not having his own query answered.

'Come in and sit down here.' She motioned him towards a large sofa-set and disappeared somewhere.

Bunny almost sank into the seat. It reminded him of his bean bag, so cushy it was! He regretted not bringing the BB with him to Chennai. In fact, Bunny was quite in the mood for reflection at that moment, and so much at home did the sofa make him feel that he was lost in thought for a while. Soon, he had plunged into the depths of slumber land.

A firm tap on the shoulder aroused him.

'I knew that your bank is a sleepy organization, but I'd never thought that you would literally sleep during our meeting!' said an attractive young lady, probably in her thirties, who stood near him.

Bunny rose with a start and apologized.

'Very sorry, ma'am! I'm Bunny Kapoor.'

'I'm Mrs. Badrinath. Would you like some water?'

Without waiting for an answer, she summoned the grim lady who had answered the door and she brought a glass full of the liquid. The grim lady gave him a frightfully dirty look as she handed it over. Bunny drank without any fuss, and apologized again to Mrs. Badrinath.

'What a terrible start to an important meeting! What if I lose Mrs. Chari's trust and also my job for this?' Bunny was clearly distraught.

Once they were finally seated face to face, Bunny gathered his wits about him and sized up the opposition. He had already learnt that she had been brought up in a well-to-do home and that she was married to a man who had inherited a large amount of wealth. What he now discerned was that she was clearly not happy at being a 'mere' housewife, and wanted to be in the thick of action, in one way or the other. By creating a scene about the 'treatment' meted out to her by Vera Bank, she wanted to find her name in the newspapers and get a kick out of that.

'Well, Mr. Kapoor? What is your explanation for the behaviour of your colleagues?' she came to the point.

Bunny was a bit wary of this 'thirty-something', considering the fact that he had been dealing only with forty-somethings for weeks. He took a deep breath, looked her in the eye and smiled before coming out with the explanation that he had been instructed to offer. She listened intently and watched him closely.

'Mrs. Badrinath, you had subscribed to the phone banking facility and when the agent took your call she was told by you to transfer rupees five lac to your husband Mr. P. Badrinath's account. She made an error by not verifying the name of your husband. I guess she thought that the 'P. Badrinath' to whom you were referring was the same P. Badrinath to whom you had transferred funds the week before that, not realizing that your husband and the other P.Badrinath had the same name. Thus, the amount was credited to the account of the other P. Badrinath and not to your husband's account. However, within seconds of your telephonic complaint two days later, the other P. Badrinath was contacted and the amount was duly credited to your husband's account. The error is deeply regretted, ma'am. It was inadvertent and not deliberate. I have come to personally apologize and to assure you that nothing of this sort would ever happen again.'

She listened with rapt attention. Ms. Grim had too joined them to listen but Mrs. B had shooed her away halfway through.

'If I agree to not go to the press with my complaint, will your bank agree to a request of mine?' Mrs. Badrinath seemed to be in a conciliatory mood. She looked at him with a gleam in her eye.

'Certainly, ma'am! Anything that is reasonable would be agreed to instantaneously,' responded Bunny, not wanting to over-commit anything.

'I want to have you as my relationship manager. Does that sound like a reasonable request?' she fluttered her eyelashes at him.

Game over!

'Sure, ma'am. I'll convey your request to my boss and also tell her that you have abandoned your plans to take this issue to the media.' He got up with these words.

'Won't you stay for some coffee?' asked she of him with another flutter of the eyelashes, as Ms. Grim walked in again. Perhaps Mr. Badrinath had engaged The Grim's services to keep an eye on his pretty wife!

Bunny smiled at Ms. Grim, who did not smile back. He got up, refused the offer of coffee and sought to be excused, with the promise that once appointed as Mrs. B's relationship manager, he would be at her beck and call.

'Very well!' said Mrs. B. 'But don't call me 'ma'am', the same is Swathi.'

She shook his hand. Her hand was warm, noticed Bunny.

'Sure, Swathi. See you soon,' Bunny walked out with a grin on his face, determined to convey the good news to Mrs. Chari without delay.

Mrs. Chari smiled at him without inhibition for the first time ever. She ordered some coffee, which arrived all too soon.

By now Bunny had begun to relish each moment spent in her company.

'Bunny, I must say that you have a way with women. Swathi Badrinath is not the sort to soften up readily. I have had occasion to meet her myself,' Mrs. Chari did not hold back her praise, for once.

'I must admit that I wasn't sure of you at first. I gave you a chance simply because of your enthusiasm and your ridiculous good looks!' she added.

Bunny Kapoor's system had felt the need to blush many a time during his life, but the need had never been as pressing as at this time. Being credited with possessing the 'ridiculous' variety in good looks was quite a compliment, especially coming from Mrs. Chari.

'Now you've displayed initiative and grit too and have emerged as a star performer for us. I'm really proud of you, Bunny!' the stream of accolades continued.

Bunny was just about to return some of the compliments, for he was a chivalrous man and she was a woman who impressed him greatly, when Shankar entered the room, his hair standing on end.

'What is the meaning of this intrusion, Shankar?' Mrs. C was not one to take agitated intruders lightly.

Shankar opened his mouth to say something but for some reason the words could not come out. He was clearly flustered. Mrs. Chari and Bunny looked at him quizzically.

Two men wearing masks walked into the room at that moment. They were carrying what looked like firearms.

'Hands up!' was the muffled command from one of them, addressed to no one in particular.

'Gosh!' Bunny's mind raced. 'I'm in the midst of a real bank robbery!'

Bunny and Shankar raised their hands as directed, but Mrs. Chari was made of sterner stuff. She walked up to one of the dacoits and gave him a ferocious slap across his masked face, thereby making him drop his weapon, more out of astonishment than anything else.

The other man predictably turned his gun towards the boss, but Bunny could not tolerate that. He pounced on him from the back and grabbed him in such a manner that the nozzle of the gun was forced to point upwards. A shot was fired, but luckily the bullet could only embed itself into the padded ceiling. Bunny shook the man violently, forcing him to drop his gun. He had no chance of escaping from Bunny's grip. Shankar, in the meantime, had recovered sufficiently from his dazed existence to throw and pin down the bewildered first dacoit. The tables had been turned!

Mrs. Chari picked up both weapons and pointed them at the dacoits, making Bunny and Shankar squirm along with the bandits. She was quite a sight, in her orange sari, with guns in both hands. The members of the staff rushed in at that moment followed by some alert looking policemen. The bank's alarm system was blaring to deafening effect. An enthusiastic media photographer was the next one to enter the already crowded room; he started clicking without much ado.

The dacoit in Bunny's arms, realizing that the game was well and truly up, fainted at that very moment.

Mrs. Chari smiled victoriously.

The next morning, the heroic feat of the threesome from Vera Bank was splashed all over the papers. The picture of Mrs. Chari with a gun in each hand pointing at the two masked men struggling under the iron grip of Bunny and Shankar was a super-hit! It was carried even by the international media and the three became instant heroes.

Each of them gave several interviews and signed even more autographs the next day. Financial rewards were announced by the Chairman of the bank. The Gang of Bank Robbers had threatened revenge, but no one was taking them seriously since their two king-pins were behind bars.

Bunny was summoned by the boss at 4 pm, after a day of frenzied activity. She wore a turquoise blue sari and looked elegant. But the look on her face was a worried one.

'Sit down, Bunny,' the boss ordered.

'Congratulations, ma'am. It was your courage that won the day for us. The staff is really proud of you.' Bunny grabbed the opportunity to convey his feelings to her personally.

'If you recall, I was telling you the same thing when we were interrupted yesterday. I really am very proud of you, and indeed of myself for having recognized the potential in you. However…' she paused as she'd done on the very first day.

This time, however, the word 'however' sounded ominous to Bunny.

'You will have to leave, Bunny! I can't have you here anymore,' she made a solemn face as she said these words.

'But why, what's my fault?' Bunny was flabbergasted.

'It's not your fault, Bunny. There are a couple of reasons, but I cannot tell you them. I request you, more as a friend than as a superior, to put in a request for a transfer to our Bangalore office. You'll save me from a major personal crisis if you do.'

She was almost pleading by the time she finished the last sentence.

Bunny was even more shocked. He hadn't a clue why she wanted him away from herself. She was looking ill at ease and unlike the Mrs. Chari who had always seemed in command.

Sending him away had obviously been a tough decision for her but one that she had to irrevocably make.

'I'll do so immediately, ma'am,' said Bunny, who knew that she would not be dissuaded. 'It would have been wonderful to work with you, under your direct control, for a while more, but I know that we will continue to meet and that in you I have a well-wisher for life.'

He looked at her hoping for a positive response; it came in the form of an animated series of nods from her, but he could also see that there were tears in her eyes, and that she was about to break down. He felt a large lump in his own throat.

'Go, Bunny,' was all that she managed to say, and he complied.

Sreedhara had just rounded off another of her soulful songs and had won applause not only from the young man sitting opposite her but also from the entire set of clients present at the up-market fine-dining restaurant when she noticed that her companion was not himself.

'Bunny, what's the matter with you? I've never seen you looking so downcast. I thought this was to be a celebratory dinner!' she questioned him thus.

Bunny could hold back no longer. He just had to tell someone, and under the circumstances, it was only Sreedhara whom he could confide in.

He told her all about his growing affinity for his boss, her recent warmth towards him, the attempted bank robbery and then the bombshell. He wanted someone to decipher the meaning of it all, and Sreedhara was just that someone.

'Don't you understand, Bunny?' explained Sree. 'She must have grown very fond of you and her husband must have sensed the extent of her feelings for you. How could she have afforded to have you around every day? It would have been very painful for her. Also, she must have realized that you were taking a liking to her and it would have been unfair on her part to not put an end to this dangerous chemistry. She must have started to feel jealous of your female accounts and especially of that Swathi Badrinath! The only way to set things right was to send you away while keeping your job intact, and that is precisely what she managed to do by transferring you to Bangalore!' Sreedhara smiled at Bunny sympathetically.

Bunny knew that Sree was right. He also knew that he himself wouldn't have stayed on for long at Vera Bank after he had attained a sense of accomplishment in the job.

He smiled back at Sreedhara.

'What would I have done without you? I was about to throw in the towel when you emerged from nowhere at the coffee-stall that day. You and Ramanathan were my saviours in this city. Thank God, I managed to convince Ramanathan to open his own account with us, otherwise I would've been totally male-less!'

They laughed heartily. Bunny knew that it was time to move on once again, but also that he had made lifelong friends in Chennai.

'What does your husband do, Sree? I've always been meaning to ask,' he finally remembered to enquire.

'He's the Chairman of Vera Bank,' said she, rather nonchalantly.

4

Bunny's On Track!

Bunny's jogging obsession was the result of a glimpse that he caught in his mirror of what looked like a paunch, though it could have been a figment of his imagination as well. So mortified was he by this that he took to running in Bangalore's sprawling green belts with a vengeance. Bunny recalled his days as a brilliant school-level athlete and realized what he'd been missing by not spending enough time on his fitness. He began jogging for at least 90 minutes each morning, and the 'imaginary' paunch soon receded in the face of such determined opposition. His long strides took him to a girls' college one day. On finding no impediment at the gate, he started jogging on the track there. After doing a few rounds, he noticed a giant of a man following suit, accompanied by a shapely damsel.

The two of them obviously didn't think too much of Bunny's running at first, for they tried to outpace him. Finding however that Bunny was no mean runner himself, they gave up and settled down to a steady pace behind him.

Bunny smiled to himself. Soon, it was time to go and get ready for work, so Bunny made his exit from the campus, but not before noticing a poster proclaiming ***Athletics Coach Wanted***.

Bunny sprinted all the way to his flat and, after due consideration, decided that he would not like to quit his cushy job to become the athletics coach at a girls' college. Yet, the thought troubled him all day. Did he really love his present job, or would he rather be outdoors on the sports field?

The next morning, his jog at the college brought him much the same results, except that this time the giant gave him a dirty look, while the gazelle gave him a pleasant smile. Bunny decided there and then that he just had to vanquish the big man in whichever way he could, and that he also wouldn't mind getting the shapely one as his own jogging partner.

He filled in the application for the post of coach that afternoon.

'You've never been a coach, Kapoor! And you don't even have a diploma in coaching. These certificates of your track and field achievements are years old and will not do! How can we appoint you here at Mayor College?' the Principal of the College was as negative and grumpy as any Principal that Bunny had met in his time.

'But I think he has potential and he's young. In any case, we do not have a qualified candidate. I feel that we should give him a chance.' This unexpected support came from an elderly gentleman who seemed to be the Chairman of the College Trust, or something like that.

The Principal was a clever man, for he shed his speed-breaker like ways upon hearing the Chairman's views.

'Of course, sir. We should give the young man a chance. Well, then, Kapoor, why don't you report next week to receive your appointment letter? Initially, you'll be on contract for six months,' he said.

He also added a note of caution.

'Do remember that this is a college for girls, and that we expect you to conduct yourself in a gentlemanly manner.'

Bunny decided that he did not like the Principal one bit, but nodded in agreement and the interview was over.

'Here goes!' he told himself as he stepped out.

Nupur was not only the star athlete of the college, she was quite a head-turner as well. She was the one who'd caught Bunny's attention during his morning jogs on the college track. And it was she who was the natural choice to hand him some flowers as a welcome gesture on behalf of the athletics team. The other girls clapped and Bunny smiled coyly. He'd better get used to being surrounded by lots of girls, he told himself.

'Right, ladies!' announced Bunny, aware that he'd better get down to business. 'Let's get warmed up for our first training session.'

The girls paced the track in a pack and Bunny ran behind them. They looked like a promising bunch, but Bunny knew that only strenuous efforts would help them win medals at the forthcoming inter-college meet. Currently, Mayor College was fourth in the city rankings, he'd been told.

A couple of rounds later, Bunny motioned the group to join him in a circle and he gave them his first pep talk. They looked at him a little warily. Bunny knew that he would have to earn their respect quickly.

'Girls, you're not just girls, you're athletes! You're bound to excel in the forthcoming competitions if you think positively and give your best. You'll never fail, on the track or off it!' Bunny gave them a determined look as he said these words. The girls cheered and clapped at this, but one of them seemed to misunderstand.

'Sir, do you think we are not giving our best? Please do not label us as shirkers.'

'What's your name, ma'am?' Bunny asked her. On being told that it was Richa, he explained to her that he was just giving them general guidelines and not commenting on their past record.

'Richa, I'm sure you're the most enthusiastic and energetic athlete in the whole team. Now, I want to see you prove it in the coming days! We're going to have internal competitions regularly.'

Richa seemed adequately pleased at this. The others gave her friendly nudges. The ice had been broken.

'Sir, will you take the winners out to watch a movie?' Nupur asked him aloud with a flirtatious smile.

'Sure, I will. But if I can beat the winners then they'll have to treat me.' Bunny smiled back non-flirtatiously. They all cheered.

The next few days were thrilling. Bunny was surrounded by pretty girls. He loved being outdoors, and felt a sense of being totally alive on the field. He planned meticulously for each day and put his wards through their paces accordingly. Bangalore's weather is world famous for being pleasant and amiable. Bunny realised that the capital of Karnataka was definitely the ideal place for sporting activities. The girls responded well after his initial sessions and he could see that they were bubbling with enthusiasm. Nupur in particular ran gracefully and with unflagging energy. She was a middle distance runner and Bunny felt that she would do superbly well in the 800 and 1500 metres categories. He wondered though whether she herself realized that she had so much talent. She seemed a little lost and distracted off the field.

'Nupur, can I have a word with you?' he asked her one morning, after a gruelling training session. 'I hope you're confident of your preparations for the upcoming competitions? I feel you can do really well in the next season.'

Nupur responded shyly.

'Sir, I'm a little low on confidence after my injury last season and I'm a little uncomfortable in your presence,' she blurted out.

Bunny was taken aback. Nupur was clearly not as focused on the task at hand as she should have been.

'Why are you uncomfortable in my presence, Nupur?' Bunny asked, though he had some idea why.

Nupur didn't answer. She looked a little bit like a school girl with a crush on her new teacher. Bunny felt uncomfortable but then realized that being the coach, he must take charge of the situation. He was also determined to check any feelings that the beautiful girl was capable of generating within him and changed the topic.

'How did you get injured?' he asked her.

She rattled off a longish story about how she'd fallen after bumping into another athlete at an inter-college event last season.

'I got back to training last month but I am still not a hundred per cent in my mind,' she concluded.

'Yes, you'll have to strengthen your mind more than anything else,' Bunny smiled at her.

She floored her coach with a dazzling smile, and Bunny realized that it might turn out to be difficult for the two of them to focus on athletics in the coming months. But he was determined to not stray this time. He was about to say something to throttle any chemistry that might be in the making between them when he received a firm tap on the shoulder from behind.

'Mr. Coach! I thought that I told you to keep your distance from the girls.'

It was the Principal and he was looking very stern. Nupur and Bunny had been standing at the edge of the ground, right opposite the Principal's window, and he had obviously been watching them for several minutes.

Bunny did not like being tapped from behind and we have already learnt that he was none too fond of the head of the college. He realized, though, that to an onlooker, Nupur and he might have indeed seemed to be having a rather cosy tête-à-tête.

But Bunny was not one to take false accusations lying down. Despite appearances, his conversation with Nupur had been entirely professional.

'Mr. Principal!' retorted Bunny in much the same tone that the other had used. 'I was discussing with Nupur her prospects in the upcoming season. If you don't mind, I'd like to continue with my discussion.'

The Principal was clearly not used to such answers. He mumbled something about the errant youth of today and the need for Bunny to keep his interactions brief in future, and stormed off. Bunny glanced at his pupil. She was glaring at the Principal's back but then turned to look admiringly at her coach. Bunny felt an unwelcome flutter in his heart. He made sure that it went away in a hurry.

'See you tomorrow, Nupur,' he said, as he turned to walk away. He saw from the corner of his eye that she was disappointed at his abrupt departure, and that gave him further cause for worry.

Bunny had bought a new bean bag and he willingly sank into it later that evening, dead tired after a hard day's work. He went over his encounters with Nupur and the Principal in his mind. Bunny knew that he could handle the Principal and that he wouldn't allow the silly man's wild accusations to bog him down. But Nupur was a different matter. Deep inside, he was still fond of his Mumbai girl, Tarana, and hoped that he would meet her again after her return from the US. The problem was that Nupur could not be easily ignored.

Bunny sighed and decided to sleep over the problem.

Days passed by in a hurry. Bunny had completely forgotten the giant jogger with whom Nupur had been running when he'd first laid eyes on her. But, one day, as Bunny turned around on feeling another tap on his shoulder, he found the said giant staring down at him. His memory thus refreshed, Bunny looked at the tapper quizzically, wondering why people kept tapping him from behind as if it were their birthright.

'Mr. Coach, what's your name then?' asked the giant of him, in a not-too-pleasant tone.

'Who's asking?' was Bunny's counter question.

'I'm Joseph. Don't you recognize me?' was the counter to the counter.

Bunny shook his head, wondering why and how he was supposed to know that this man's name was Joseph.

The giant glared at him, clearly displeased at not being recognized and seemed quite unhappy at Bunny's very presence in the college.

'I'm Joseph Pinto, the champion athlete of the garden city. I'm on page 3 every day. Don't you ever read the papers, Coach?' The giant snarled and hissed as he said these words. He stepped closer to Bunny with the apparent aim of frightening him with his sheer size and copious venom.

Bunny Kapoor was made of sterner stuff than it had apparently appeared to the giant. He stepped even closer to the aggressor and looked him straight in the eye. He didn't like the way the man was behaving, and he was not fond of being addressed as 'Coach'!

'If you're such a star athlete, Pinto, then why aren't you on the sports page? Why page 3?' Bunny's response was steeped in sarcasm.

The giant flinched but did not move an inch. Both men retained their positions and also their aggressive intent for what seemed like an eternity, before Bunny felt yet another tap from behind. He turned fearing the worst, sure that both the Principal and Pinto had ganged up on him. He found the lovely Nupur smiling at him instead.

'Sir, meet Joseph, my ex-boyfriend,' she said, brightly. 'He's just returned from a visit to the United States.'

Both men took a couple of steps back. The toughest of males are prone and known to soften up in the company of females of Nupur's pedigree.

'I still don't know his name,' complained the giant, somewhat mildly.

Bunny realized at that moment, for he was a smart cookie, that a big oaf like Pinto could not be defeated by antagonistic methods. He must try other means, for he knew that there was a need to neutralize not only the challenge posed by this new adversary but also its possible implications.

'I'm Bunny Kapoor. Nice to meet you,' was the introduction that he proffered, hand outstretched.

The giant hesitated to shake it, but a quick glare from Nupur shook him into action and he did the needful.

'Welcome to Mayor College, Mr. Bunny Kapoor, Coach!' he said finally, and even displayed the hint of a crooked smile.

Nupur's arrival clearly had a salutary effect on both men for they shook hands yet again. Bunny walked off to the training area, leaving the two of them to catch up. He turned to look at them from afar and noted that there was a lot of animated hand movement involved in their conversation. The former boyfriend was clearly losing the argument, for his massive shoulders were drooping. Finally, Nupur left the man standing there, and jogged towards her coach.

'I wanted to ask you something, sir. Would you be free to join me and my mom for dinner next Saturday?' she enquired upon arriving in his vicinity. She looked as pleasing to the eye as ever, even in a track suit.

But Bunny was determined to avoid unnecessary off-the-field contact with Nupur and to focus on the job at hand.

'Unless it's a special occasion, Nupur, I'd prefer not to. Once you've won a couple of races I would gladly celebrate with you and your mother, but no socializing right now. How are you feeling about the big race next Saturday?'

Nupur looked downcast but eventually smiled.

'Very well, sir. There's nothing extra special that day; I was just keen to have a chat with you over dinner. A few weeks later then! I'm sure to win those races!'

She seemed to be getting bolder with him for she winked as she said this.

'Well, I'm happy to see that your confidence is sky high!' said Bunny, ignoring the wink. 'You'll definitely do well. You're in good shape and in the right frame of mind, but watch out for over-confidence. It can be a deadly enemy.'

She looked at him with respect. Anything that he did or said seemed to impress her.

'Yes, sir; I'll watch out!'

The other girls joined them now and the practice session began in earnest.

Bunny worked as hard as he could, putting in the extra effort himself to ensure that the girls followed suit.

Bunny was wary of the Pinto factor for the next few days, though the giant was nowhere in sight. He was obviously a man who got what he wanted and was clearly not used to being overshadowed. His boast about Page 3 was not an idle one either. His pictures were in the papers quite often.

Bunny himself was proving to be a hit with the girls of Mayor College. Not only the athletes but even students from all groups would come up to him and greet him. The teaching staff had grown fond of him too. His wards looked up to him and they were putting in their level best under his eagle eye. Bunny was able to point out to each girl a couple of basic improvements that were necessary in their techniques. The results would be evident in the forthcoming meets, he was sure.

The day of the season's first big event arrived and Bunny was all charged up. Seven of his wards were participating in the meet being held at a neighbouring college. All seven qualified for the finals, with Nupur's time in the 1500 meters being the best in the field.

Gloria from Mayor's team won the 200 metres final and Bunny exulted. His first gold medal as a coach!

Nupur came to seek his inputs on her race and he advised her to keep pace with the leaders for the first couple of laps but to keep sufficient reserves for the last 'kick'.

'Sure, sir!' she replied, 'and I'll keep in mind the bit about 'positive energy' too!'

They smiled at each other, and she went off to run.

Bunny looked eagerly at her, but his attention was distracted by the sudden appearance near the track of Joseph Pinto. For reasons best know to Pinto, he walked over to Nupur at the starting line and whispered something in her ear, as a result of which, a look of anguish appeared on Nupur's face. She held her head for a while and kept shaking it thereafter.

The line judge blew his whistle and all the contestants trooped to the starting line, except Nupur, who was still looking distraught. Bunny was about to rush to her side, when he noted that she had finally decided to take her position. He waved at her and gave her a thumbs-up sign, but she continued to look distracted and gloomy. Whatever it was that the giant had said to her, the news wasn't good and the timing was worse!

Bunny decided to accost Pinto and give him a piece of advice about what to tell women and when to tell it. Before he could do so though, the race began with the sound of a shotgun.

Nupur's race turned out to be a disaster! She trailed the pack till the half way stage, and just gave up thereafter. The winner lapped her and she came in last. Bunny threw his cap to the ground in disgust.

He walked up to Pinto in a hurry now, and held him by the collar.

'How dare you disturb my athlete just before an important race, you oaf!' Bunny was in a fiery mood.

'Take your hand off my collar, you loser! I'm not answerable to you for anything,' Joseph Pinto was not one to back off from an argument.

Bunny had not punched anyone in the face in years; he decided that this was as good a time as any, so he let his right arm fly. The giant was quicker than he appeared though. He swerved away and easily avoided the blow. Pinto was about to land a big left of his own onto our hero's ear when he received a high impact missile on his cheek. Nupur's hand had connected with the surface of Joseph Pinto's face in a real hurry.

People turned to look at the three of them as they stood in positions that were straight out of a comic book fight. Pinto was the first one to move. He looked sorrowfully at Nupur, avoided glancing at Bunny, and was on his bike even before one could say 'spoil-sport'. Nupur in turn evaded Bunny's gaze and walked slowly towards her car. Bunny was left standing there to fend off curious eyes.

The next morning, Nupur had a reason to avoid her coach. She was plainly ashamed of her performance in the big race but she did not want to discuss the cause with Bunny. However, Bunny caught hold of her after practice and confronted her.

'Young lady, I can make out that you're in distress, but then so am I! As a coach, I need to know what affected your performance so dramatically that you ran such a terrible race. Come on, tell me all!' Bunny demanded.

'Sir, please don't force me on this. I cannot tell you what Joseph said to me. But whatever it was, it disturbed me so much that I could not concentrate. I'm really sorry, sir. Do give me another chance,' Nupur pleaded.

Bunny was puzzled. He knew that he had to get to the bottom of this, else Nupur could say good bye to medals for the season.

'Listen to me, Nupur,' he said. 'If that loafer Pinto is going to disturb you before important events, you've had it for the season, and I will not allow that to happen! I don't want to know about your personal problems, I just want to ensure that you run as fast as hell, without having your mind burdened. Now tell me how we can avoid such situations in future.'

Most men know that women are unpredictable, and Bunny Kapoor was one such man. He wasn't prepared for what was to come though.

Nupur put her hand in her pocket and pulled out a photograph. It was one of her with Pinto and their pose in it was a little intimate. Bunny stared at it wondering why she'd given it to him. She answered his thoughts.

'He was blackmailing me about that picture. He said he would show it to the Principal and to my family.'

'The rascal!' Bunny was livid.

Nupur nodded and Bunny saw the light.

He realized that life often presented before him situations in the face of which he just had to respond in a heroic manner. It wasn't that he was on the lookout for conflicts, but then he also wasn't one to let a rogue harass a fair damsel if he could help it. He made up his mind to teach the blackmailer a lesson.

Bunny did not, as a habit, break into people's houses, but that night he entered Joseph Pinto's through an open window. Treading in pitch darkness into a large room, he wondered what Pinto did for a living, apart from blackmailing people. The house was rather large and well furnished. Only the rich can afford such luxury, thought our man.

He could hear some snoring in process in another room and on peeping furtively in that direction, Bunny discovered to his satisfaction that the snores were indeed emanating from the Page 3 person of Joseph Pinto. In the dim glow of the night-light, one could see that the giant was alone. A sleeping duck, whispered Bunny to himself and smiled.

Pulling out a cardboard megaphone from his satchel, Bunny proceeded to put his plan into effect.

'Joseph Pinto! Wake up, you blackmailer!' Bunny shouted into the improvised instrument, sounding more like a buffalo than a human being.

Pinto did not stir at first but, after a second or two, he turned groggily towards the source of the sound. He was half awake.

'Who...who's there?' was his query in the dark.

'Do not attempt to get up from your bed or your head will be severed from your body, Pinto! Now, listen carefully. This is a message to you from your conscience. Do not blackmail anyone or you will vanish from the face of this earth!'

Pinto was wide awake by now. He made half an attempt to spring out of bed, but on knocking his head against the table lamp, thought better of it. He looked suitably dazed.

Bunny had gambled upon the fact that Pinto would not have much common sense and would probably be a coward at heart, like most bullies are. He was proven right without doubt in the next thirty seconds.

'But who are you and why are you here?' Joseph Pinto's voice quivered as he asked these perfectly valid questions. Anyone who is woken up in the middle of the night by a strange voice would be similarly entitled!

Bunny grabbed his chance.

'To make sure that you understand the law of the universe, Joseph Pinto, that is why! Now listen! You must forget Nupur and never contact her again. Also, you must stop blackmailing people in order to save yourself from dire consequences.'

He tried to sound as terrifying as he could. Pinto was eager enough to comply anyway. He probably thought it was a nightmare.

'Of ccc…course!' he stammered as he spoke; he confessed all. 'You're right. But my ex-girlfriend Nupur is the only one whom I've ever blackmailed. That too because she's getting too close to that new coach. I hate that man's guts! If you so command, I'll forget about her immediately. I've found a new girl anyway!'

Bunny almost collapsed in mirth at this unexpected subjugation by Pinto, but retained enough composure to come up with one last warning.

'Be warned! Unless you do so, you will suffer great agony and pain! You will never be able to walk again! Do not dilly-dally! Now go back to sleep, you are safe!'

Bunny heard a sigh of relief from Pinto. He was such a dodo!

'Thank you, thank you!' was all that Pinto had to say.

As he crept back to the window, Bunny heard footsteps from the far side of the building. His heart skipped a beat and he almost dived out of the window, knocking over a lamp that fell with a loud clang.

'Now I've had it!' He felt his heart thumping.

A burly figure caught him by the arm as soon as he slipped out of the window. He didn't know who it was. Perhaps Pinto's father, for he was similarly built. Bunny took a big swipe at the man's nose with his right. This time, the punch connected and the senior Pinto's voice rang out loud and clear in the silence of the night.

'Ouch, thief! I'll get you for that!' he shouted. But Bunny had broken free and run off.

The senior Pinto must have been an athlete in his time too for he gave a spirited chase while calling out his son's name in the hope that he too would join in. But Joseph was out like a light.

Out onto the pathway, then into a park and finally onto the main road, Bunny increased his lead.

Finally, Bunny left the much exhausted and exasperated fatherly giant bending over in the middle of the road trying to get his breath back.

The next morning, Bunny was smiling and whistling while running a few laps with his team. The girls wondered what had gotten into him.

Nupur was in the dark too, for Bunny had not shared with her any detail about his plan or its execution the previous evening.

After a while he pulled her aside.

'Listen to me carefully. Joseph Pinto will not come near you again and you can focus on your races without fear.'

She looked at him in bewilderment.

'How do you know? And what makes you so sure, sir?'

'Whatever the reasons, he won't bother you, so just do as I say,' he winked at her. 'Now run along and prepare for the mock race.'

Nupur nodded, winked back and complied. She had just left when Bunny heard a whisper in his ear.

'Quite a romantic scenario that, Mr. Kapoor!'

The Principal, who had a knack of appearing unexpectedly, had cropped up out of the blue once again.

'There's no romance here, sir, just pure professionalism. The college won one gold and two bronze medals at the last meet, and we're going to improve upon that at the next one. You'll have no occasion to discuss anything but our performance on the field as the season progresses, I can assure you.' Bunny was defiant.

He looked the Principal in the eye, and the latter decided to retreat. Not without leaving behind a barb though.

'Well I do hope that you're right, Coach. That girl Nupur does not seem to be focusing on the track of late.'

Bunny almost reacted to that statement, but he realized that his results should speak louder than his words, and he held himself back once again.

As he sunk into his bean bag at the end of the day, he decided that the Principal too needed to be taught a lesson.

The most significant event of the season was being hosted by Mayor College and it was a chance for Bunny's girls to better their performance. The big day arrived and saw Bunny all excited and animated. He rushed across the field several times before the official opening. Though he was chiefly responsible for the on-field activities, he was also assisting the organizational team in last minute preparations.

The Principal strode about looking important and without a doubt feeling the same. He finally took a position near the entrance and awaited the arrival of the Chairman of the Trust who was to declare the meet open. Bunny avoided him for the time being. He would wait for the right moment to act.

Nupur and the other girls were busy warming up, as were the athletes from other colleges. A sizeable crowd was building up.

Bunny received a warm handshake from the Chairman once he arrived but the Principal only looked at him with annoyance behind his boss's back. Bunny just smiled back. He needed to focus on the races for now.

Bunny's motivational skills were more responsible for the success of his wards in the short time that he'd been in charge than his technical inputs. Nupur was one of those who really needed a dose from him today. Pinto was conspicuous by his absence but she could not take any chances, given her disastrous outing the last time around.

'I'll repeat what I said earlier. Just focus,' said the coach to her. 'Do not think about who's watching and what's going to happen if you win or lose the race. Just go out there and give your best!'

Once the race began, Nupur kept pace with the leaders and then surged ahead halfway to loud cheers from the home crowd. The best was still to come though—she put in a phenomenal effort in the last 200 metres to win the gold medal by some distance. Bunny was ecstatic and he jumped up and down like a little boy, as did Nupur's team mates. She ran up to him and he gave her a high five.

'You were stunning out there, girl! I'm delighted for you. I knew you could do it.'

Nupur was smiling very broadly and had tears in her eyes.

'I couldn't have done it without you, coach,' she held out a hand, and Bunny grasped it.

'You can win every race that you run, girl!' Bunny's eyes were moist too. After all, Nupur was a very talented athlete in addition to being special.

Their conversation was interrupted at that point, this time not by the Principal but by the Chairman standing next to him.

'My boy, Bunny! I'm really proud of the way you have instilled in these students the right approach to competing in top level events apart from the technicalities that you must have obviously worked on. Congratulations and I'll make sure that you get an early raise for your efforts!' the Chairman patted Bunny on the back as he said these words.

'I'm off now, but I'm going to announce a fee waiver in honour of all our gold medallists of this season. Well done!' he concluded as he walked off.

Bunny knew that his moment had come.

'Sir, I'm really grateful to you for the encouragement. Can I have a word with you alone?'

The Chairman nodded and the Principal was left with no option but to withdraw to the sidelines.

It is not known what exactly Bunny said to the Chairman, but he had his ear for almost 15 minutes. By the end of their conversation, Bunny was smiling. The Chairman, however, looked grim and the Principal, very jealous.

'What did you tell him, Kapoor?' the Principal wanted to know when they crossed each other.

'Wouldn't *you* like to know!' Bunny exclaimed.

He turned to see that the Chairman was giving the Principal a real dose, for they were both going red in the face as the Chairman spoke and the Principal listened.

As the meet progressed, Bunny's girls continued to shine. He clapped his hands above his head to egg on the sizeable home crowd. There were loud cheers and the atmosphere became extremely buoyant. By the end of the day, Mayor College had won 5 gold and 2 silver medals!

'Mayor! Mayor!' was the cheer that went up. Bunny's girls gathered around him after the medal ceremony and lifted their coach high above their heads!'Bunny Sir! Bunny Sir!' was the loud chant that emanated from their lips. Nupur was the leader of the pack and she was back to being her exuberant self.

Bunny's face turned crimson. Being held aloft thus by several pretty women was not an everyday occurrence in his life. There were not too many highs that could compare with it!

Bunny looked around the room that he was the sole occupant of. His gaze had just stopped at the sight of a funny looking clock when an imposing figure walked in.

Nupur's mother was not a woman to be taken lightly. She was as imposing as Attila the Hun. Their conversation had barely begun when she bent forward to look Bunny in the eye and offered him another *idli*.

'Do I sense that my girl is attracted to you, Mr. Kapoor?' she asked, giving him an intimidating look, as if her daughter's condition was his fault.

Bunny was trying to negotiate some piping hot *idli-sambhar* in his mouth at that moment.

He took his time to respond, mulling over the exact words that he should use as he chewed on the food. Nupur's mother did not move back an inch in the meantime.

'I thought so too for a while, ma'am, but then it's a normal phenomenon when it comes to coaches and trainees. However, with some firm hints from my end, she seems to have controlled her feelings.'

Bunny looked carefully at the lady's face for her reaction.

The formidable figure moved back and relaxed in her seat. She finally smiled at him a whole twenty minutes after they'd been introduced. Nupur walked into the room, carrying some more *idlis* and *sambhar*.

Bunny had come over for a celebratory breakfast session. A dinner invitation had been ruled out by Nupur's Mom.

Bunny was not complaining. The *idlis* on the menu were delicious and he'd polished off a dozen of them already.

As Nupur sat down to join them, her mother came out with the quote of the day.

'Handsome men are aplenty, but honest ones are as rare as tigers. Keep that in mind, Nupur. I like your coach.'

Bunny almost choked on his next *idli* when he heard these words. He needed a firm pat on the back from the senior lady to regain his composure. Nupur had fetched some water from the kitchen in the meantime. Bunny gulped it down gratefully.

'You must concentrate on what you're eating, Mr. Kapoor. There's no point in letting your mind meander at such times,' was her advice to him.

Bunny knew he must be careful with his words here.

'Thanks for the compliment and the advice, ma'am. I'll be moving to Kolkata soon and I do hope to keep in touch with Nupur and you.'

The effect of this statement on mother and daughter was predictable. Nupur started wailing like a baby as her imposing Mom got up from her sofa with great agility.

'Girls like Nupur are hard to find too, my boy! She's not only beautiful and talented, she also has a heart of gold.'

Bunny realized that he'd been duped into considering a marriage proposal for which he was not ready. He decided to take matters in his own hands.

'Ma'am, with all due respect, Nupur should not get married for another five years. She should run for the country and win medals! Rare talents like her are hard to find. In any case, I'm not ready for marriage yet. I would like to wait a while.'

Nupur's' wails got louder and her mother had to shut her up. Attila moved closer to Bunny, who had no option but to stand up too. One problem with that was that he was probably not going to be able to gorge on any more *idlis*.

'Quiet, Nupur! I do not give up easily, Mr. Kapoor. I will chase you down wherever you go.' She glared at him from close quarters once again.

It was at that moment that Bunny saw a picture of Nupur's Mom hanging on a wall opposite him. He wondered how he'd missed it. She was a police officer!

Bunny wondered whether she would pull out a gun next. He must change tactics immediately.

'Ma'am, you will not have to chase me. I will come and meet you a year from now and we will then decide. There will be more clarity by then.'

He moved a step back as he uttered these words. Nupur's mother made a face at him and stood motionless. Bunny felt as though he was face to face with death itself. It took an eternity for her to withdraw.

'Alright, Kapoor. We will meet next year on my 50th birthday and, by then, I hope I will have your decision!'

Bunny glanced in the direction of Nupur who seemed to have cheered up in the last few seconds. He wondered how he'd landed himself in this mess. But this was not a time for confrontation. It was a time for diplomacy.

'Sure, ma'am, anything you say! I'll be here for your golden birthday and we will decide then.' One year seemed like a safe zone to Bunny. Problems are known to sort themselves out over such a long period.

Nupur's mother smiled broadly at this, then picked up an *idli* and thrust it into Bunny's mouth. He accepted it gladly hoping to not end up choking again.

'Take care, young man!' said the policewoman, as Nupur smiled gleefully and Bunny thanked his stars.

After he'd packed his bags the next day, he wrote out a note for Nupur wishing her luck and asking her to concentrate on her running.

He'd learnt that Pinto had moved to Mumbai. That should help Nupur to focus on the track, Bunny thought. The Principal too had been replaced by a genteel lady, Mrs. Joshi. The Chairman had obviously taken Bunny's feedback seriously.

All was well at Mayor College. Bunny had a song in his heart and a spring in his step. He would need that spring during the next few months.

5

Bunny Moves Deftly!

Kolkata is an extraordinary city with a rich tradition of culture and heritage. Classical music is taught to girls and boys from a young age as religiously in modern times as it was taught in centuries gone by.

A section of the youth of Kolkata has also taken to new-fangled mores quite readily. Bunny was made aware of this fact immediately on his arrival at Dum Dum airport. The student who received him was hip and pretty. Her name was a very foreign sounding 'Xena', though she looked like a typically charming Bengali girl. The clothes she wore were straight off the pages of fashion magazines and she spoke with a sense of urgency at all times.

'So, Bun, how was the flight? Can't wait to learn some new salsa moves from you, Hon!'

Bunny was used to being called 'Kapoor', 'Mr. Kapoor', 'Bunny' and lately 'Coach'. He was definitely not used to being addressed as 'Bun' or 'Hon'. He was also not used to being talked to so informally by a total stranger.

'I can't wait to teach you either!' was the enthusiastic response from him.

'Great to know, Bun. I've heard that you're a real whiz on the dance floor. I'm so looking forward to this! Come let's go before the office rush takes over the Kolkata roads.'

There they were, seated in a black car with no roof, in the face of Kolkata's heat, with Xena at the wheel and Bunny at her side, speeding along in the midst of some already dense traffic. She drove like the wind. He was wondering whether he should address her as 'Xee' to reciprocate, when she suddenly broke into a song. Predictably, they had some narrow misses along the way. He shut his eyes tight several times as Xena narrowly missed knocking people, cycles, carts and animals down en route to their destination.

All this while, Bunny was forced to listen to her full-throated rendition of a Hindi film song, the words of which can be roughly translated as '*Save yourselves, pretty girls!*'

Is your song a warning to the pedestrians on the road? I can't see too many girls though,' Bunny ventured to ask her.

'Oh yes it is, Hon! I always drive like this and I love to sing this song on the way.'

Bunny sighed and braced himself to handle three uncomfortable factors for the next 90 minutes—Xena's driving, her singing and her habit of 'Bun'ing and 'Hon'ing him. The heat and humidity were nowhere in the running.

Being in an utterly helpless situation, as human beings often are, Bunny resorted to praying as the only means available for dealing with the crisis.

When they finally arrived at Groovy Academy, the venue for Bunny's next career shift, they were greeted by a dozen youngsters. Most of them seemed to be Xena's friends for as soon as she stepped off the car, she hugged them all. Bunny wondered whether she was something of a celebrity, and whether he had unknowingly missed acknowledging the fact.

'Thanks very much, Xena, for taking out time to pick me up and to drive me here,' Bunny shook her hand as he said this.

'Oh, it's been such a pleasure, Bun! You said such wonderful things to me. Take care and I'll see ya soon.'

With that, she got back into her black beauty and sped off singing another song that Bunny could not quite place. He wondered which 'wonderful' things she meant.

'Right then, Bunny Sir! Let's go inside!'

A deep voice owned by a tall thin youngster invited him thus inside the building. As Bunny walked up the stairs, he realized that the premises of Groovy Academy had probably seen better days. The stairs were chipped at places and the walls were not in very good shape either. The Academy was obviously a bit under the weather.

The lanky youth led him to a room where behind a small desk sat the smiling figure of Debashish Chatterjee.

'Debu!' Bunny greeted him with a hug.

'Bunny, how wonderful to see you! Welcome to Kolkata!' Debashish beamed at him.

They had been pals in college but had lost touch for years until that fateful evening at Brigade Road, Bangalore, when he had danced all night with his trainees. Debashish happened to be there on a trip and was at the Night Club too. They had exchanged notes and Debashish had offered to get him a job in Kolkata as a dance instructor. Debashish knew how fleet-footed Bunny had been on the floor during his college days.

If he needed any reminding, Bunny's performance that night did the trick.

Everything thereafter worked out well and here Bunny was – at Groovy Academy, looking forward to working with his old friend and also shaking a leg with some energetic learners.

'We're going to meet the Chairperson tomorrow, Bunny. You can settle in the apartment that we've booked for you. It's walking distance from here. But first let's have some coffee.' Debashish was warm, but businesslike. He rang a bell, asked for coffee and soon they were both sipping some.

'Thanks for everything, Debu. I'm here because of you. And thanks even more for getting me a place nearby. If I had to be driven to work by Xena every day, I would have lost all my hair!'

They laughed at Xena's driving, her singing and her other quirks.

'But mind you, Bunny, she's a star of sorts here,' Debashish informed Bunny.

'I gathered something of the sort myself, Debu. But if she's so good with her moves, what can I teach her? She seemed keen to learn...'

'Bunny, my boy, life is all about creating the right impressions! I've managed to hype you up so much that these kids are eager to be part of your core group. They're all talented, and not one of them is a beginner, I can tell you that. But you're good enough to handle them. I know you well enough, Bunny Kapoor!'

Bunny smiled at his old chum, Debu, but wondered whether he would indeed be able to hold his own with the likes of Xena in this latest arena.

His first day on the job was neither without entertainment nor incident.

The elderly looking paan-chewing Chairperson was a warm but pre-occupied lady. She painted for Bunny the macro-level picture.

'Welcome to Groovy Academy, Kapoor. We have high expectations from you. We want to ensure that the Academy draws the best talent and also that our financial position improves with more admissions. We will depend on your performance and popularity a great deal!'

Bunny nodded, decided that he liked her and made up his mind to help elevate the Academy to great heights from the depths into which it seemed to have plummeted. He loved a challenge and here was a massive one! He would have to do his homework well. He planned to incorporate the latest global trends in his western dance classes and, for this purpose, he decided to update his own skills by watching dozens of videos and practicing hard.

Bunny's introduction to the ongoing batch of trainees was an event in itself.

Debashish praised him in glowing terms before them and made his exit. Bunny asked the group, about twenty in number, to introduce themselves with a dance step each. Some peppy music was already being played in the hall. Xena was the first to step up. She made an elaborate set of moves and generated many oohs and aahs. Bunny watched her in awe. She was a great dancer, much better than he himself was. He'd better be wary of her.

'Thanks, Xena. That'll be all. Let's have the next person on the floor,' Bunny was keen to show that he was in charge.

Xena gave him a somewhat surprised look, but smiled and did as told. The next one was a laugh-riot—he jumped up and down like a jack-in-the-box. His ample girth created quite a noise and almost a dent in the floor. One by one, the class showed their stuff, and Bunny felt relieved that except for Xena, he could indeed handle them all.

Itching to take the floor himself, Bunny swooped on to centrestage and danced for about five minutes accompanied by deafening applause. The group was impressed beyond doubt. One of the girls even joined him on the floor. Everyone smiled and cheered. The mood was set, and all appeared in order.

Except that Xena decided to faint at that moment.

There she was, standing and clapping, when all of a sudden she fell as if lifeless. To worsen matters, she hit the floor with a thud which did not sound at all good. He rushed to her side and so did a few others. They managed to lift her onto a bench, and Bunny realized that she was not lightweight despite her alacrity as a dancer. All attempts to revive her failed. One of the youngsters made the mood darken even more when he wondered aloud if she had breathed her last. Bunny gave him a glare and instructed someone to fetch Debashish immediately so that they could get her to a hospital.

It was at that moment that Xena opened her eyes and got up with a start. She found a worried looking Bunny staring at her from close quarters and promptly gave him a big hug and a loud kiss on the cheek. All present cheered loudly.

'Thanks for saving my life, Bun! I almost died...dunno what happened, but everything just went black!'

She stood up amid protests from Bunny and the others, who wanted her to rest for a while, but she shrugged them all away.

'I'm fine, folks! See, I can dance too!' she seemed quite sure of herself and even executed a little jig.

Bunny was confounded by this mercurial Kolkata girl and walked out after mumbling a word of thanks to the students. He went straight to his new address, had a bite, and fell off to sleep without much further ado.

It was not often that Bunny Kapoor remembered dreams of nights gone by. He was thus startled to find that he could recollect vividly a longish but unpleasant dream when he awoke. As he sipped some coffee, thoughtfully provided for at 7 am by Debashish's attendant, he realized that Xena had affected his mind powerfully. The problem was that, as opposed to the usual romantic effect that most beautiful women had on him, Xena's was a nightmarish influence.

He'd met her only twice, but for some reason she had managed to impact even the inner recesses of his mind. He couldn't still get over being called 'Bun' and 'Hon' by her. He also felt uncomfortable at having been kissed and hugged by her in front of the class. He was not used to that sort of thing in public.

His nightmare was full of such Buns and Hons and kisses and hugs. He'd hated them.

'Come on, Bunny, pull yourself together. She's your student not your girlfriend!' he told himself, determined not to let her occupy so much space in his mind.

He walked to the Academy at noon, reached at the designated time, and parked himself on a chair opposite the desk belonging to Debashish.

Debu was not in yet, so Bunny leafed through a newspaper to while away his time. He was astonished to find an item in the local pullout with the heading *New Dance Head at Groovy*. The item went on to mention his name along with that of the Chairperson. It was the last line that made his eyes really widen though: '*Xena, the dancing sensation of Kolkata, is among the students enrolled for classes at the Academy*.'

Bunny sighed. This Xena would not let him think of anyone or anything else.

He walked into the hall a few minutes later and found that his students were all in attendance, including Xena.

'Right folks! Let's begin with our first salsa lesson. I want each one of you to pair up with a member of the opposite sex, ASAP!' Bunny got straight down to business.

As luck would have it, there was only one extra girl, and that happened to be Xena. All the boys seemed wary of pairing up with her. Bunny realized that he was not the only one scared.

'I guess I'll be dancing with you, Hon!' Xena walked up to Bunny.

'Yes, Xena, but I would prefer to be called Bunny and nothing else, whether in class or anywhere else,' he said to her, moving a little closer, so that the others could not hear him.

'Sure thing, Bun, let's dance!' Xena said, and with that she caught hold of him, and, before long, they were hand in hand, arm in arm, and grooving to loud screams and whistles from the class.

They were very compatible on the floor, their movements gelling well. Xena's 'Cuban' hip movements were rather elaborate and Bunny realized that she was an exotic dancer. They kept upping the energy levels till they were both drained.

The onlookers were whistling loudly by now. Bunny felt relieved when they finished, to deafening applause. He was keen to dispel any speculations of a permanent pairing with Xena by choosing someone else the next time.

She seemed pretty happy with herself though, and came up to Bunny to whisper in his ear the following ominous words:'I think we were hot together, Bun. You'd better watch out for me!'

Bunny simply smiled in return, quite mechanically.

He walked away from her and asked the students to step up according to their pairings and execute on the floor what they had learnt in previous classes.

Some of the couples were quite good, others were so-so and still others were quite pathetic, noted Bunny.

Bunny realised that one of the girls was a close second to Xena and quite attractive too. Bunny grabbed his chance and went up to her.

'What's your name? You can dance with me in the next round,' he said as he neared her. He was determined to get Xena off his back.

'Himani, sir. I'd be glad to dance with you. Thank you!' was the girl's confident and smart response.

The whole routine was repeated, with the pairs being asked to observe Bunny and his new partner in action. The new girl was much lighter and easier for Bunny to dance with than the weighty Xena. He liked Himani's smile too.

Xena was forced to dance with Gary who had earlier paired with Himani. She didn't look too pleased; Gary was a very tall guy who seemed slow of foot and still slower of brain.

Gary seemed uneasy while dancing with Xena and Bunny smiled as he watched them. Xena was obviously too much to handle for a normal guy. Her whole personality, her exaggerated movements and her energy made her akin to a hot-potato.

When the class finally ended, Bunny decided to take his students out. They cheered at the idea.

'We'll have to go Dutch guys! I'm not rich,' Bunny said sheepishly.

A new night club had opened in the vicinity and since it was past 8 o'clock, they dashed there for an impromptu bash.

Bunny was the first one on the floor and, after partaking a few drinks, the whole gang joined in. Bunny never touched alcohol, but found it amusing to see the group in their true colours.

Xena was quite a guzzler and so was Himani. The men were all inebriated by 10 pm. The result was that the representatives of Groovy Academy turned into a noisy lot as the evening progressed.

Bunny was fine with their boisterousness though; by getting to know them better, he had already met his target for the evening. He was not prepared for what followed, however. It may have been the liquor or perhaps it was just the simmering rivalry.

It started off when Bunny was dancing with Xena and Himani wanted a turn with him. Xena left the floor in a huff and Himani made her seethe even more by smiling at her mockingly. Bunny quite enjoyed his dance with Himani. Xena's patience gave way after ten minutes and she decided to take matters literally in her own hands. Bunny had never been the *raison d'être* of a catfight but there's always a first time and this was it for him.

Before he could react, the two ladies had him by one arm each. He wondered if the slaves of yore had ever been tortured like this. His arms almost came off, so hard did Xena and Himani pull.

Bunny's shirt got torn in the process and he even suffered a few unintended blows as the two spitfires spewed venom at each other. The students and other guests at the club were stunned as Bunny was whirled around like a toy while the two warring parties went for each other hammer and tongs.

Realising that no one was likely to rescue him from this potentially unending battle, Bunny actually put his foot down. As luck would have it, his shoe landed on Xena's foot and she was forced to let go of Bunny!

Bunny pulled his arm away from Himani too and the two girls were left glaring at each other. Despite being aghast at the treatment that had been meted out to him, Bunny gathered the courage to summon them to a separate room for a dressing down.

Once inside he let them have it! The class huddled around to view the proceedings through a glass window.

During the next twenty minutes Bunny used words like 'shameful', 'ridiculous', 'pathetic', 'uncouth' and 'expulsion' liberally to make Xena and Himani realize the extent of their misbehaviour. They had their heads bowed throughout. It was Xena who finally spoke.

'Sir, I apologise to you from the core of my heart and I also apologise to Himani. It was I who started the fight and I am at fault more than she is. But please don't expel us, sir.'

Bunny raised an eyebrow at this unexpected response from the fiery Xena. Himani had no option but to follow suit and regret aloud her behaviour. Bunny made them shake hands and the three of them emerged from the room into the main hall of the night club to loud cheers from the class.

Bunny did not want the party to end like this. He signalled his students towards the floor again.

'What are we waiting for, people? Let's get back to doing what we're good at!'

The students cheered and clapped, with Xena and Himani even hugging each other for good measure.

Bunny shook his head in amusement and amazement.

'Curious are the ways of the fairer sex,' he said to himself.

Before Bunny knew it, weeks had flown by. It was time for a concert!

The class had been practicing hard, and Bunny was preparing to leave for a dress rehearsal one evening, when he heard a knock on the door of his apartment.

Expecting it to be the milkman (he wasn't sure why the man delivered milk so late in the day!), he shouted the usual words.

'Come in!'

In walked Xena, dressed suitably for the rehearsal, but an entirely unexpected visitor under the circumstances. She had kept to herself of late and Bunny had gotten used to her.

She was no longer appearing in his nightmares, so life was finc.

But what was she doing here? Bunny got up from his sofa with a start, and looked downwards to check if his clothes were in order. (Bachelors are not used to women walking into their room unannounced.) They were in order.

'Bun, I have a bone to pick with you. Why would you have Himani on stage for more time than you'd have me?'

With that poser, and without any further preliminaries, Xena sat down on a chair in the sparsely furnished room that served as the living room, the dining room as well as the drawing room in Bunny's quarters. Her dress was ornate and it flowed on to the floor from the low seat. She looked quite exquisite, but was obviously in an offended state of mind.

'Xena, you cannot walk into my place like this! You should have asked for an appointment and I would have met you in the office.'

'I don't care for appointments, Bun! I want more of the stage on Saturday, and I know that I deserve it!' Xena was clearly in no mood for niceties.

'Listen to me, Xena! I will not tolerate a student of mine walking into my apartment without permission and then dictating terms to me.' Bunny was in no mood to buckle.

That Xena was a crazy one, Bunny knew. That she would resort to violence with him, he did not.

In a flash, Xena picked up a glass of water that had been blissfully lying on the table and flung its contents onto Bunny's already washed face.

We are aware that Bunny was no stranger to drinks being thrown at him, normally by his girls. But then Xena was not his girlfriend!

However, Bunny was not one to retaliate where women were involved. He shook his face to rid some of the wetness, walked towards the door, opened it and said just two words.

Xena was in no mood to comply. She was in a real temper and seemed capable of both further violence and a flood of tears. Bunny was not sure which but he feared both.

She stood there staring at him with the empty glass still in hand, her body trembling with fury. Bunny stared back, but without trembling.

'Alright then, Mr. Bun Shun!!! I'll show you how a dance school should be run and let's see who's more popular! You watch out, man!'

Xena thus pronounced her drastic designs. They may have been cooking for a while, but Bunny was surprised. She stormed out, but not before giving him a terrifying glare, one that shook him to the core. Never in his life had Bunny met a woman quite as daunting as Xena, the famous dancer of Kolkata!

The show was a runaway hit. People cheered from all kinds of positions. Some stood on their chairs while dancing, others fell off them.

The crowd was so delighted with the performance that some of them ran towards Bunny, Himani and even Gary for autographs.

Xena had opted out and had already announced in the papers her plans to launch a new school of dance. Bunny had given a chance to a young but talented girl Bonita in her place. Himani and Bonita had shone beyond description and Bunny was overwhelmed. He had been training these kids for just 4 months, and they were already better than many pros.

Bunny himself had performed during the grand finale and had a dazzling sequence with Himani at the very end which had left the crowd breathless. Himani had given him a huge hug as the curtain had come down and Bunny had to utilise all his resolve to break away.

Debashish and the Chairperson were ecstatic and rushed to congratulate him and the class. Bunny received more hugs from all and sundry and was compelled to climb down the steps in order to avoid being crushed.

A special desk that had been set up to enrol new students recorded the receipt of 438 applications. Groovy Academy was truly rocking now!

They partied hard that night and Bunny danced as if he had wheels in his shoes. Even the Chairperson shook a leg, so elevated was the mood.

The next morning, Bunny was pleased to see a huge report in the main English daily, accompanied by a spectacular shot of Himani and himself. He noted the widespread coverage that the other papers had accorded to the Academy too. Several critics had showered praises.

Bunny smiled, satisfied that he had just conquered another bastion.

He was about to put away the glossy section when his eyes fell on another picture, one of Xena addressing a press conference. The heading said *'Groovy Academy played foul with me'* and the item went on to criticize Groovy's management and Bunny. Xena was also quoted as saying that she was all set to start admissions for her new school to be called 'Xena's Arena'.

Bunny wished her well in his mind and shut his eyes. He could snooze for a while more before reporting for work to welcome the new batch.

Bunny's fame spread far and wide. Mothers dressed in elaborate saris and their daughters dressed in bare minimums visited him by the dozen for admissions. Groovy Academy became known for quality and class and the management was thrilled to bits.

The problem was that they could accommodate only five

batches per day but the demand for admissions was far in excess. Bunny would screen applicants personally and take on board only those who could dance well already and who were the cheerful sorts. He did not want grumpy people any more.

The result was that the disgruntled many who were denied entry to Groovy found shelter in Xena's Arena. Her stock grew rapidly too and Xena's picture stared at Bunny from the pages of one or the other Kolkata daily every week.

He often recalled their last meeting when she'd barged into his apartment, had ordered him around and had thrown water at him. He was proud of himself for having shown restraint that afternoon.

Recent graduates of Groovy were now doing superbly well in films and TV shows but then so were some of those from Xena's academy and the latter got more mileage in the media.

The problem for Bunny was that he was not as media savvy as was his competitor. He was not unduly worried as Groovy was still ranked as the number one academy in the city. Still, he realised that the rivalry with Xena's Academy was not good for Groovy's health.

He felt that there was a need to bring Xena back to the fold somehow so that the two academies could work together. Debashish agreed with him. Very soon they had a plan.

At the next award ceremony for those who had successfully completed courses at Groovy, Bunny planned a gala show for which he invited dancers from other academies including Xena's. Not surprisingly, all rivals except Xena's Arena accepted the invitation. Bunny decided to be patient. Xena knew Groovy's shows were the best in the city. She would be desperate to be involved.

Sure enough, Xena called up Debashish one day and expressed a desire to participate with her troupe.

The stage was set and the glitterati of the city gathered at a plush hall in south Kolkata with the media in full attendance.

Xena's students were to perform the penultimate item whereas Bunny's team was to begin and round off the show. The hall was packed and the crowd boisterous. They danced in the aisles to the peppy numbers and cheered loudly as the groups came on stage.

Xena ran onto centrestage in dramatic fashion when her turn came. Her troupe put up a quality performance with Xena herself hogging much of the limelight. Bunny noted as he looked on that her dream of performing on the big stage had come true at last and she was obviously loving all the glory associated with it.

Bunny and his wards were all set for the grand finale. A glowing and breathless Xena crossed him as she left the stage to rapturous applause.

'Hey, Bun! I owe you a million apologies. Wow! I loved the cheers that I got. You invited me tonight despite our recent tiffs and I'm bowled over. You're a gem, thanks a ton, Hon!'

The hug that Bunny received from Xena almost spoilt his attire but he knew that he had won over his *bête-noire* with tact and could henceforth sleep in peace.

Bunny and his students scorched the stage with an electrifying item that left people gasping for more. Leading the cheers were former students of Groovy like Himani and Bonita. All troubles forgotten, the dance world of Kolkata had come together like never before.

Strange are the ways of fate. With fences mended, Groovy soon entered into a tie-up with Xena's Arena. The two academies decided to work together for promoting dance in the city. Joint events were organized and they soon were a rage among the youth of the metropolis.

Bunny became a Page 3 personality for the first time in his life and he was often spotted at parties. The list of influential people calling him up for the admission of youngsters grew longer.

The Housewives Batch at Groovy was a superb success. Most married women preferred to enrol there in order to boast at kitty parties that the dashing Bunny Kapoor was their teacher.

One such housewife became quite enamoured of him and started calling him up at odd times. Bunny would have none of it. He ticked her off and she backed off for a while.

But when the grand finale neared, she got a politician to give Bunny a call for she wanted the lead position with him on stage. On being summoned and told firmly by Bunny that he would not tolerate any interference, she settled down again.

Groovy's mega-show was once again a superhit and Bunny became the toast of the social circuit in Kolkata.

At the post-event party, Bunny was almost mobbed but managed to survive and smile throughout the evening. He felt on top of the world. Debashish and he joked and laughed so much that their stomachs began to hurt with the effort.

A tallish man walked up to Bunny past midnight and introduced himself.

'Hi, Kapoor! I'm Ruben Pal, Chandrika's husband. I make films and I want to cast you in the lead role in my next one.'

Bunny's ears popped. He had never dreamt of having anything to do with films. Agreed he had worked at a multiplex, but a 'filmy' role? Never!

This man was obviously a brave-heart though for Chandrika was the pestering housewife whom Bunny had been trying hard to avoid. The fact that Ruben Pal had survived her all these years was testimony to his qualities of head and heart. Bunny decided to at least find out what kinds of films he made.

'Probably tear-jerkers!' was his guess.

To Bunny's surprise, Pal's response was not in the realm of the ordinary.

'I make films about the supernatural. My next film is called *Dance Like a Phantom*. Would you like to play the lead role, that of a dancer who starts sleep-dancing after nightmares?'

Bunny almost choked on his mineral water.

'No, no, Mr. Pal. I've no talent for acting save in the face of real life predicaments. Please consider someone else!' Bunny was quick to come out with his excuses lest Mr. Pal consider this bizarre plan seriously.

'I know you're very modest, Kapoor. My wife's been praising you to the skies. Do give me some dates in September at least!' Much like his wife, Pal was not one to be shaken off easily.

'Doggedness runs in the family,' Bunny figured.

Bunny was about to put forward a second set of imaginary reasons for not accepting the role when Pal did the unthinkable. His right hand dived into his pocket and emerged instantaneously with a contract as his left hand held out a fountain pen of the finest variety.

Bunny was gobsmacked by the man's gall. He looked left

and right for a saviour. Xena was standing near the bar, regaling some youngsters with hair-raising tales.

'Ah, that's it. The two are made for each other.' Bunny walked towards his former-student-turned-rival-turned-friend with great speed, followed very closely by Pal.

After quickly reaching Xena's left ear, Bunny whispered the needful into it.

Xena listened carefully and turned to find Pal breathing down Bunny's neck.

'Oh, Mr. Pal, I'm so grateful for your offer! I would love to play the role of a sleep-dancer in your woman oriented film. Here, let me sign up.'

She took a step forward to grab the sheet of paper even as Pal took two steps back and Bunny took many steps towards the exit. He did not turn to look back. The last sound he heard in the room was a cry of anguish from Mr. Pal.

In the next day's papers Bunny was raved about and celebrated as a genius, as someone who had revved up the entertainment industry in the city.

He was even mentioned in one glossy as being a very eligible bachelor with dashing good looks. Bunny didn't like the picture that went with that item though. It was one of his worst ever.

He stood up with a start at this last thought. Was success going to his head? Was he acquiring the airs of a spoilt celebrity? *I hope not!*

He suddenly realized that he had after all managed to reach the pinnacle of glory in the glamour circles of Kolkata. There were not too many peaks left to scale here.

Xena could easily take over from him at Groovy! He would

recommend her name himself. The management was bound to agree. The two academies could even merge into one under her leadership.

It was time for him to head homewards!

It was not easy for Bunny to say good bye to Kolkata. Ruben Pal accompanied by his wife and some former students chased his car all the way to the airport in a last ditch effort to persuade him to stay.

Fortunately for Bunny, his driver was once again the lightning quick Xena. So, while he did lose a bit more hair on the way, he managed to catch his flight well before the fans caught up.

As he sat on the plane he thought of the last words that Xena had uttered while kissing him good bye. He wondered if he would miss her, after all.

'Adieu, Bun! Thanks for getting me the role and also for asking me to head Groovy! Have fun, Hon!'

6

Speak Up, Bunny!

Bunny's flight was rather smooth. It landed punctually at the Delhi airport. He looked forward to devouring home-cooked food that evening. It had been a while since he'd been home to meet his parents. Now that he was planning to work in Delhi again they'd be happy to have him around.

His Dad had developed health problems of late and Bunny was certain that the senior Mr. Kapoor's morale would be significantly boosted if his cheerful son were with him for a while.

He collected his bag and was planning to join the longish queue of pre-paid taxi-seekers when he saw a placard sporting the mystifying name 'B. Kapoor'. The bearer was the smiling sort and as Bunny walked a step towards him in wonderment, the man approached him hurriedly.

'Mr. Kapoor?' the man asked him, quite unsurprisingly for one carrying that particular placard.

Bunny nodded and was about to inform the man that he had not been expecting anyone to pick him up when his bag was pulled away from his hand with great force. The man was already running towards the exit with it and Bunny had no option but to follow suit.

His hurried shout of 'Wait!' was inaudible to his receiver in the din and even before Bunny could catch up, the man had a swanky car at the ready.

'Get in, sir, there's very little time!'

Bunny was almost sure that it was not him that the man had come to pick up but then his name was indeed 'B. Kapoor' and he had not been asked for any credentials, so he hopped in. He was not complaining!

'Maybe one of my admirers from Kolkata has organised the vehicle!' he thought to himself and chuckled softly.

The man drove off and was on the phone for almost forty minutes, the duration of the journey. Bunny and he had no exchange of words apart from one quick sentence from the other.

'We're almost there!'

'What have I landed myself into?' Bunny wondered for the first time, quite sure now that it was all a mistake.

The car entered a driveway and pulled up with a screech at the porch of a largish building where the door was opened by a comely sari-clad woman who seemed more than a little tense.

'Mr. Kapoor,' she said quite breathlessly. 'You're just in time.'

With those few words, she turned and sprinted down the corridor. Bunny wondered how tough it must be to run in a sari and rushed after her to explain that she had the wrong Kapoor.

He caught up with her at a doorway and opened his mouth to speak, but she abruptly handed him some papers and walked inside. Bunny followed as he glanced at the papers. They were about some seminar on '*Rapid social changes in modern society.*'

When he looked up, he found himself standing behind a podium on a stage facing an audience of about two hundred people.

'Ladies and gentlemen, I present to you, Mr. Kapoor himself!' the woman announced in a melodious voice before she withdrew with an engaging smile.

Faced with a major crisis, Bunny was paralysed, rooted to the ground and scared as hell.

He shook himself violently to gather his wits, thereby toppling the mike over with a clang.

A man emerged from nowhere, saluted him and straightened the object.

Bunny looked at the crowd. As of now, no one was laughing at him or even smiling. They were all looking at him in a polite sort of way and waiting patiently for him to begin.

His wits were in danger of un-gathering themselves again so he repeated the shake-yourself routine, this time without disturbing the mike.

'I must tell these people that I am not who they think I am or I've had it!' he said to himself.

He was sure that the real B. Kapoor was at that moment standing in the queue for pre-paid taxis at the airport.

He turned around to see the charming woman standing behind him with an eyebrow half raised. Bunny realized that the moment was not far when the said eyebrow would attain the lofty position of being fully raised.

He turned again towards the audience just in time to see that certain eyebrows in the first row had commenced their upward journey too.

Bunny knew he had just a few seconds before people would catch on and start throwing tomatoes at him. The fact that none of them appeared to have tomatoes in their pockets did not occur to him at that harrowing moment.

He made his decision and began his speech.

'Ladies and gents, I'm not the outstanding Kapoor whom you think I am but I'll do my best!'

For some reason they all clapped at this confessional opening and did not realize that something was seriously amiss. Bunny was certain that the other Kapoor was a whiz and a renowned scholar. He wondered whether he'd be able to fill even the toes of his shoes but he continued speaking.

'Our society is changing more rapidly than any other in the history of the world!'

The audience applauded as if Bunny had just divulged a great secret. His blood began to circulate once more. (The paralytic attack of a few moments ago had all but stopped the flow.)

'We need to pause, people, we need to think, and we certainly need to take stock!'

Bunny's voice was loud and clear now. Those present evidently liked what he said and clapped even more enthusiastically. Bunny took a sip of water from a small conference-type bottle and continued.

'Our children need to inherit an earth that is not only safe and healthy but one that is also inhabited by good human beings!'

The audience cheered at this. Bunny looked around and saw his hostess clapping too. He began to feel at considerable ease as a result. He continued to speak in an uncharacteristic manner. Perhaps the mike had brought out the orator in him.

No one seemed to notice that he was not coming up with any real pearls of wisdom. He guessed that he must have been a leader of sorts in previous births, for his speech flowed effortlessly. After twenty minutes he was ready to wind up.

'We, the men and women of today, must realize that unless we channelize the flow of this change, unless we make sure that society progresses in the right direction, we would fail in our obligation to future generations. I seek your wholehearted cooperation to ensure that the world becomes a better place to live in! Good luck and good bye!'

Bunny was not sure whether to have another sip of water at that point or to forget it and just run for the exit. His dilemma was resolved by the standing ovation that he got. The audience was overwhelmed, it seemed. Bunny was pleasantly shocked. He had said nothing worthwhile in his speech but people had relished it. He decided to have a sip.

He also decided to keep up the façade and to ad-lib his way out rather than admit that he was the wrong guy.

People who flocked towards him to ask questions were dissuaded by the woman who had received him. They were asked to email their queries to her instead.

'I'll pass the questions on to you, sir! Should I use the same email id that we corresponded on earlier?' she asked him.

'Er…no. Please use oratorkapoor@gmail.com!' Bunny thought that one up on the spot.

He then asked her where the restroom was. Once inside he heaved a sigh of relief.

'My God! That was nerve-wracking! I wasn't bad with the speech though. I wonder if they pay for these sorts of things.'

He emerged a little later. The little-miss-efficient was there again, smiling at him.

'I didn't get the chance to tell you that you look much younger than I'd expected. Here is your honorarium for today, Mr. Kapoor. It is in cash. Apologies for the paltry amount but it is all that the institute can afford!'

Bunny peeped into the envelope to see a few thousand rupee notes neatly stacked therein. He figured that the profession of delivering speeches was not a bad one.

It was against his values to pocket this particular money though. It was meant for someone else.

'I want to donate this to the institute's welfare fund. Can I?' he enquired, handing back the packet to her.

The woman's eyes lit up and she took it gratefully.

'Mr. Kapoor, I admire you so much! You're so gracious, and what a speech! I'd heard so much about you but you were even better. And the audience loved it!'

Bunny was about to respond when he noticed a taxi pulling up at the porch and he wondered if the real Kapoor had arrived. It was time to flee!

'Ok thank you, ma'am!' Bunny shook her hand, noticed his bag lying at the entrance, grabbed it and walked away briskly. A red-faced man carrying a matching briefcase was walking in at that moment. This was surely the real Kapoor!

'Why didn't you send me a car?' the man shot at the woman without indulging in any preliminaries. Bunny did not wait to find out what her response was. He made his way with alacrity through a crowd of people who were still leaving. Once outside the main gate he looked for a taxi but found an auto-rickshaw. He hired it and commenced his homeward journey.

He realized that he'd forgotten to ask the woman her name. But that would have to wait!

Bunny's father looked up at him from his newspaper the next morning. He'd received a warm 'Welcome home!' the previous night and had eaten so much that his stomach had almost burst. His mother's cooking was the best in the world, he was sure. He had to take several digestives before he felt better.

He had just told his father over a cup of morning coffee that he intended to become a motivational speaker, causing his father to pull away his attention from his beloved newspaper for a minute.

'Really? But you cannot make a living out of being a speaker! In any case, you have no experience,' Bunny's father said to him.

Bunny had heard the bit about having no experience many times before in his life. But that had never deterred him from traversing unfamiliar territories.

'Dad, I'm not a teenager any more. I know what I'm doing. I've been successful in all the jobs that I've taken up till today. It's just that after a while I get bored of each one and begin looking forward to new challenges.'

His father frowned and said with fatherly concern, 'I know that, Bunny! There is no doubt about your capability. But you should settle down to a career now instead of shifting around so much. When you called from Kolkata you were a dance instructor or something!'

Bunny smiled back at him.

'Dad, you know me well. I cannot settle down to anything for very long.'

His father sighed, and relented.

'Alright, son, go ahead and become a speaker. Let us know when you want us to attend a talk of yours. We'd love to.'

Bunny's eyes moistened as he smiled at him. His mother had been listening in and took her chance.

'And what about settling down with a life-companion, son?'

Bunny smiled sheepishly at her. This is a ticklish topic with most families and Bunny's was no different.

'Oh, come on, Mom! I'm only 26. I'll let you know when I find someone!'

Bunny spent the whole day scouring the internet for opportunities as a speaker. He realized that he would have to build an image and also have an impressive CV before people began inviting him. He would also need to select a couple of topics on which he could speak with relative ease. Style was important but so was substance after all. No one would call him on the basis of one inspirational talk delivered at an event where he was not even on the list of speakers!

Despite feeling a little morose as a result of these thoughts, he created the new email id that he'd given to the sari-clad lady at the seminar. What if he became a renowned speaker and actually needed it one day? With that happy thought he sunk into his bean bag and slept soundly in it all night.

Bunny was not expecting any emails in the 'Orator Kapoor' account but by the next evening he'd received seven of them, all from the same efficient girl. Her name was Niyati. The first five had been forwarded by her from admiring listeners; one was from her own self and the last from poor Mr. B. Kapoor!

The appreciative members of that day's audience were full of praise in their missives and minced no words to tell him that he was the next big thing!

One of them actually wrote the following-

'Your command over the language and the manner in which you waxed eloquent on a subject of great complexity were astounding, especially for one so young.'

Bunny smiled. His heart beat faster as he opened Niyati's email.

'Sir, I'm not sure what your name is but you've received rave reviews from all present for your speech the other day. The media has also covered it extensively. I do realize that the car driver and I were very abrupt with you but you could have told us that you were not Mr. Bhuvanesh Kapoor! Anyhow, I handled the real man tactfully and gave him the amount that was graciously returned by you to compensate him for the trauma caused.

All I can say is that you never seemed out of place on stage and if you drop in some time we might have a coffee and a laugh or two!'

'What does she mean by "real man"?' wondered Bunny, jokingly. 'I'm a real man too!'

He chuckled and decided to take up her offer for two reasons. Firstly, he never refused an offer of coffee from a pretty girl. Secondly, she might actually invite him to speak again if she had been so impressed.

On the other hand, Niyati could also get him arrested for impersonation. But he was ready to risk that eventuality.

He clicked open the last email. It brought tears of laughter to his eyes.

'Mr. Who, you have some nerve! You stole my car and then my limelight. Now I'll have to go around explaining why my head is bald and why I cannot speak with the same verbosity as 'I' did that day. After all, that speech you delivered is recorded in my name.

I'm told that you escaped moments before my arrival. A case should be registered against you for deceit! What I cannot fathom is why you left the money behind. You are an enigma indeed!

Although I can use your email id to track you down, I will not do so for I am busy and have a dozen speeches lined up across the country during the next fortnight.

I wish you well but do make sure that you speak for yourself in future!'

'These speaker-types are quite barmy!' Bunny said to no one in particular for no one was present.

He then stood on his chair with a pencil that served as a mock mike to 'broadcast' a warning: 'Watch out all you eminent speakers. Here comes Orator Kapoor!'

Bunny was seldom nervous during a meeting with anybody. The sari-clad young lady seated across him looked prettier than the other day but she was no Greta Garbo. Nor was she intimidating. In fact she was the giggling sort! Bunny's anxiety was entirely due to his previous encounter with her.

She ordered coffee and got down to the point.

'You know what, Mr. Kapoor, I've never laughed as much as I did when the real Mr. Kapoor turned up! He was so cross with me and there I was, unable to suppress my giggles. That infuriated him and I laughed even more!' She giggled for about eight seconds as if to demonstrate the way in which she had giggled.

'No wonder he sent me that threatening email!' Bunny thought to himself.

Niyati looked at Bunny's business card. All it said was 'Bunny Kapoor'.

'So your name is B.Kapoor too; no wonder the confusion occurred! It was really good of you though to deliver the speech once I'd introduced you. I would've felt like such a fool had you not done so!'

'Well under the circumstances it was to be either me or you so I volunteered to be the fool of the day,' Bunny explained.

'Trust me, Bunny, except for the first few seconds when you'd dropped the mike and had hesitated a little, you were extraordinary! In fact you were so good that a few people called up the next day to invite you to their events as a speaker. What's your topic of interest, Bunny? If you like I could line up a few more speeches for you. Only you'd be speaking as yourself this time!'

She giggled again and Bunny decided that she was cute and that he liked her. Bunny looked up at a plate on the wall which stated that she was the Deputy CEO of the Institute, a position which seemed a tad too senior for her.

He was excited by what she'd just said and confident that he had not erred in deciding to take up speaking seriously. The fact that he didn't have any particular area of specialization did not deter him. Niyati could be of great help.

'I can speak on anything really, except perhaps astrology and ornithology! I can address youngsters on career options for I've explored quite a few myself. I can also give pep talks to almost anybody. I was quite good at them when I was an athletics coach.'

Niyati stopped smiling for the first time and even looked a bit worried. She looked at the wall behind Bunny and remained quiet for a minute. Then she finally looked him in the eye and came out with an offer.

'Let's start you off with some general life-skills talks to a few college level students who attend courses here and next week there's a senior citizens' forum which you could address.'

Bunny was unsure whether this sounded promising but he nodded and looked straight back into her eyes.

'Sure I'll do that and in the meantime I would send you my CV along with a few topics which I can handle with ease.'

She looked pleased at this and was soon back to her giggling self. The coffee arrived finally and the mood lightened up.

'You know what, Bunny? I'm going to write about the circumstances in which your first speech was delivered when I pen my autobiography one day! I hope I have your permission!' She came up with her most cheery laugh yet.

Bunny was only too willing. She was his only ray of hope at that moment.

'Only if you promise to keep that Bhuvanesh Kapoor away from me!'

She laughed so much at this remark that she spilled coffee all over her desk. And some on to her clothes as well. Bunny the gentleman leapt to her aid but she declined the offer.

'Oh I do that all the time, Bunny. Don't bother. I have to run for a meeting now but I hope to see you tomorrow at 5 pm for your talk.'

She extended a hand and Bunny shook it. It was sticky with coffee. Bunny looked at his hand and smiled, making her blush.

He left without another word. He would save up his talking for the morrow.

The youngsters loved him. He was energetic, on-the-ball and with-it. He knew their pulse and he knew how to make them laugh. The one-hour interaction in a small class room was like a breeze and very soon it was over. College going kids seldom let a new teacher settle in easily, but Bunny was given an unprecedented round of applause at the end of his talk.

He had floored them with statements like, 'If you think you can conquer the world one day, you're right! Sure you can. The only obstacle along your path is your own self belief or the lack of it. Conquer your fears and you will win every time!'

Bunny spoke like a pro and inspired them with his words and his manner. As he walked towards Niyati's room later, he wondered how he'd managed to come up with all the punch-lines and from which corner of his brain all the *gyan* had emanated. He was born to be a speaker! Perhaps he had finally found his true calling! Niyati was all smiles as usual.

'Bunny, you're a gem! I just had a couple of students visit me after the class and they were thrilled with your talk. I think I should put you in touch with as many organizations as possible, for the more you speak the more experience you'll gain. Soon you'll be the toast of the speakers' circuit in Delhi, mark my words!'

Bunny was happy to let Niyati do all the talking now. Everything she'd just said was exactly what he'd wanted to hear. He was keen to address as many forums as possible. He would then earn a regular income and his stature would rise steadily too.

Niyati repeated her coffee-and-giggles routine and they had a few more laughs before Bunny headed home. He had quite enjoyed his day as a motivational speaker, especially since there had been no identity fiasco involved that day!

Bunny walked once more into the institute's hall with some trepidation. He now stood at the very spot where he'd landed in a spot on the first day.

The audience this time was restless. Bunny knew that senior citizens can be hard to please. He was nervous once again but he got down to his hour-long task right away.

He decided to adopt a humble approach.

'Ladies and gentlemen, I'm not here to preach. Some of you are former bureaucrats, others former army officials, still others ex-bankers and corporate top-shots. There is nothing that I can say that you do not already know. All I aim to do in the next 60 minutes is to elevate your mood, for each of us needs mood-elevation at times.'

Bunny noticed that a few high and mighty types visibly relaxed after this opening. One gruff looking senior was keen to interrupt, however, even at this initial stage.

'What if our mood does not need your inputs, Mr. Kapoor? We might be better off without listening to you!' The man looked stern and difficult as he glared at Bunny from the first row.

'Pardon me, sir, but you're the one who needs a mood-change more than anyone else in the room. I would only request you to give me a chance,' Bunny was direct and even defiant in response.

The man seemed to have been a boxer in previous births, or maybe in this one, for he got up from his chair and charged towards Bunny, causing the latter to take a backward step or two. A couple of good Samaritans got up with the agility of men much younger and grabbed him. They pacified the 'boxer'. One of them even said some encouraging words to Bunny that made him feel better.

Our hero swung into action thereafter and went on to first build up his credentials, then to make his audience smile and finally to have them cheering at his every word. He walked into their midst carrying a cordless mike, played the fool once in a while, told them several stories and charmed his way into their hearts. He even touched the feet of the 'boxer' and won him over.

It was quite a battle, but he emerged from the hall smiling and victorious. He had impressed a difficult audience with a little bit of luck, lots of pluck and plenty of sincerity.

Some oldies caught up with him at the exit and patted him on the back, as is their wont. He felt like a school boy being congratulated by his teachers for topping his class.

One aged looking woman who reminded Bunny of his great grandmother even gave him a warm hug. Some senior citizens told him that they wanted him every fortnight and that they were ready to pay for his talks handsomely.

Niyati was not in office that evening, so Bunny went straight home and spent the evening regaling his parents with anecdotes from the eventful day.

Bunny's big moment arrived sooner than he'd expected. It had only been a month since he'd landed and announced himself so drastically on Delhi's speaker circuit. He didn't know how Niyati had managed it, but here he was walking up to deliver an address before the crème de la crème of Delhi's society on a hackneyed yet ever-relevant topic, '*Stress management*'.

The venue was South Delhi's most prestigious auditorium. It was full to capacity. Bunny experienced a now-familiar bout of nerves as he stepped on to the stage. He knew that if he is able to make a success of this one, he would really be in business. However, if he ends up messing it up, he would be more or less finished.

The fact that an electric wire had unscrupulously blocked his path did not come to his notice, so focused was his mind on the challenge at hand. The result was that Bunny went sprawling on all fours and almost ruined his clothes by colliding with a cup of tea that someone had left on the stage for no apparent reason.

Predictably, there was much mirth in the hall at his fall. The effect of this unfortunate mini-episode on Bunny was that he lost the plot. He totally blanked out and forgot what he'd planned to say. In fact he'd forgotten the topic itself. He was not in the habit of carrying notes so he had no papers to consult. Turning around to try and find it on the back drop yielded no gainful results either. All that was mentioned in bold letters was 'TODAY'S SPEAKER – BUNNY KAPOOR'.

Bunny shook himself violently. It was becoming a habit with him when in crises. He recalled vaguely that the talk had something to do with the problems of life in today's world.

Bunny was not a spiritual man by habit but his heart was in the right place and he now realized, as he had done on many occasions earlier, that praying to God was all he could do. Having done that, he started his speech without further ado.

'People! I'm going to take the liberty of altering the subject for today to "*Life as it should be led*"'

Some people looked at each other in surprise but no one objected. Niyati stared at him and gulped but Bunny did not wait for any further reaction from anybody.

'None of us has time today for our own selves. We spend so much time trying to seek happiness that we forget just that—how to be happy. We are in the midst of a mad race to reach somewhere and we forget to enjoy our surroundings and live each moment to the fullest,' Bunny started off thus.

'Consider my dramatic fall a few moments ago. So intent was I on reaching the mike and starting to speak that I did not notice the wire. I crash landed because my eyes were closed to my present environment.' Bunny was now in full flow.

'That's what ails us folks in this 21st century. We keep looking towards a tomorrow that never comes and forget a today that is so beautiful!'

Bunny paused for effect at this stage. Niyati took the cue to begin the applause. It proved to be a contagious act. To a man, the crowd applauded. Bunny's was an electric beginning.

There was no stopping him after that. He would recount true stories from his own life and stop for several seconds each time in order for the cheers to build up. Bunny had learnt, very early in his life as an orator, how to play to the gallery.

Niyati gave him a thumbs-up sign when he was three-fourths through and Bunny just went to another level thereafter. Not even great world leaders have been able to connect as intimately with any audience as Bunny Kapoor did with his that evening.

'Gentlemen in the hall, I want each of you to recall the last time that you presented your wife some flowers,' he said suddenly, causing males in the hall to cringe in their seats and their companions to glare at them complainingly.

Bunny turned the tables on the females quickly though. He could not afford to annoy 55 per cent of his audience!

'And ladies, I want you to recall the last time when you cooked your husband's favourite meal.'

This led to protests from some women.

'We work too! We come home late and have no time to cook!'

Bunny was quick to pounce on these words.

'That is precisely the point that I'm trying to make to you folks. We have no time for our own selves or for our loved ones in today's helter-skelter era!'

He paused again and stared one by one at a few pretty ladies seated in the first few rows, causing them to turn pink. There were advantages of being a speaker that he had not realized earlier.

'The fact is, ladies and gentlemen, that we do not realize what our number- one priority is. What do we live for? Inner happiness and joy! But do we find time to savour the joys that life presents to us?'

Bunny smiled and looked a few more people in the eye at this point, both men and women.

There was a hush of great significance in the hall. Niyati and a few media persons were busy taking notes at a furious pace. Camerapersons had suddenly found him to be of sufficient merit to get up from their seats and start clicking.

Bunny decided that it was time for the climax.

'Now ladies and gents, we're going to do exactly what we should have done every day of our lives. We're going to shut our eyes for five minutes and think about where our lives are headed and what we can do to improve them! Your time starts now!'

Bunny held such total control over the onlookers that even the photographers and the security guard at the exit complied with his command.

Indeed, Bunny's were the only eyes that were open as his watch ticked. He wondered at himself, at how he'd managed to hold sway over 500 people. He loved the feeling and wanted to capture it for posterity.

He jumped off the stage and grabbed a camera to start clicking. No one moved. He took several pictures of his audience with their eyes shut as they mulled over the directions in which their lives were headed.

Five minutes of silence passed and he was ready to close his talk.

'Open your eyes, please! Now tell me—did my talk help you to open your eyes to the way your life should be led?'

A young man in the fourth row stood up to clap. Everyone joined in, even the media. The effect was rapturous.

Bunny felt as if he'd won a game of chess using a brilliant feint.

'Thank you very much!' he said with a flourish and jumped off the stage in rock star fashion.

They mobbed him. He autographed at least a hundred bits of paper. He posed for photographs and received hugs and kisses from strangers.

It took Niyati 12 minutes of pushing and shoving to reach his side.

'Oh Bunny! You're a star!' She gave him a bear hug and immediately whisked him away towards a waiting crowd of TV persons and print media who were accompanied by a dozen more cameramen than he had noticed earlier. He wondered where they had cropped up from.

Bunny gave his first ever interview and they loved him. One female reporter even requested him to pose with her for a picture. Bunny blushed.

Niyati handed him a small piece of paper. He read it with some astonishment.

'I am resigning from my post to become your full-time secretary.'

Bunny's father subscribed to three newspapers. He had never seen his own name printed in any of them, neither had he expected to ever find his son's name in them either.

He almost spilled tea onto his pyjamas when he saw Bunny's photograph staring at him from Page 3 in one of them. The accompanying news item had the bold headline '*New Bunny captivates Delhi audience*'. The other two publications had similar coverage.

Not normally given to excitement, the senior Mr. Kapoor shed his inhibitions and leapt from his chair to run to his son's room knocking over a few items on the way.

'Hey, you! How can you sleep like a baby when you're all over the papers?'

He shook his son to wake him up. Bunny's mother walked in as well.

Bunny stared bleary eyed at the picture of him surrounded by dozens of autograph seekers. Even in his current sleepy state he could make out that one of the papers had spelt his name as 'Kapor'.

His parents were delighted at the coverage. He got a hug from his dad, an unusual occurrence, and one from his mom.

'Why didn't you tell us last night when you returned? I would have read the papers before my morning walk,' complained Mr. Kapoor.

'Dad! That's precisely why I didn't! You'd have woken me up at 6 am!' Bunny grinned at them, happy to be home with his parents to savour a moment of personal triumph with them.

He took Delhi quite by storm. There were invitations galore. Not only to give speeches but also to attend society events.

There were times when as many as four speeches were to be delivered in a single day. His father suggested that Bunny would do well to become a politician, having gained so much experience in public-speaking.

Some of those who were hitherto favoured as speakers in Delhi receded into the background. It was Bunny all the way, all around. He wondered sometimes from the stage if his rivals had hired goons to throw rotten eggs at him. He scanned the crowd carefully at such times for tell-tale signs. That was his only fear, none other. He needn't have worried. Only accolades came his way.

Making speeches was not like work. It was like a walk in the park for Bunny. The only tough part was negotiating Delhi's traffic in his dad's old car. He sometimes arrived late for his talks as a result.

His personal calendar was now well and truly under Niyati's control. She practically ran his life. She was not only his secretary, P.R. agent and promoter, she was also a guide and mentor to him.

Bunny knew that he could not have made it this big without her support. It was she who had pushed him onto stage in the first place, albeit mistakenly!

His effortless, humorous way of winning over audiences, his gift-of-the-gab, his charm and his good looks were all factors that had propelled him to the top of the unofficial rankings for star speakers in Delhi. No one in Delhi seemed to mind that Bunny's talks contained very little hard facts or technical content.

The media loved him. They quoted him regularly. He was even nicknamed '*Bunny the charmer*' by one paper.

Months sped by. His popularity skyrocketed. His fans ranged from school boys to grandmothers. Bunny felt on top of the world.

Niyati was a star of sorts too. She was interviewed by the media and feted for being the woman behind *the man*. There were even some uncomfortable questions regarding their relationship from pesky reporters. Nothing serious existed between them though and nothing damaging was actually reported. In any case they were both unmarried, so there was no room for scandal.

Bunny was not interested in Niyati *that* way. She was a friend and associate but nothing more. He was happy to note that she did not display any romantic inclinations towards him either.

Bunny's mother had given him a year to find a girl and settle down. Somehow she too did not find Niyati suitable, perhaps because she always spilt coffee when she visited their home, or perhaps because Niyati was too much of a control-freak. No mother wants her son to be dominated by his wife.

All was well.

Until Bunny felt that he was going too fast. He wanted to cut down on his speeches. Niyati wanted to increase the number. There was a basic difference of opinion.

An argument ensued and Niyati won it. Women normally do. Bunny reluctantly agreed to go as per her advice.

But his patience wore out a day before the international summit that he was to address. The theme of the summit was 'Happiness' but Bunny was feeling low himself.

Niyati and he were staying at a quiet little guesthouse near the venue of the event, several miles off central Delhi. Niyati had gone to her room and turned in early. She had advised him to do so too.

Bunny tried to sleep but was unable to. He decided to go and watch a late night movie. The attendant had told him that a new multiplex had come up in the vicinity.

He dressed and softly treaded downstairs. The lights were off and the attendant nowhere in sight. Finding the main door locked Bunny went back upstairs and decided to slip out of his room's window. He found a ladder to lead him down to the front lawn.

It may have been his lack of preparedness or perhaps it was the extent of the darkness but he did not see a telephone wire and tripped over it. The thud with which he fell onto the police car parked below was loud but not loud enough to wake up either Niyati or the attendant.

The only one whose sleep was disturbed was the Inspector dozing in the car. He dashed out of it in a flash and, on finding that Bunny's fall had damaged the vehicle's roof, lost his cool.

The fall had not hurt Bunny. It may either have been the angle at which he landed or the suppleness of his limbs but he was only a bit dazed from it.

The slap behind the ear from the battle-hardened veteran was tougher to handle though. The lights went off in Bunny's head instantaneously.

Waking up with a sore head in a police lock-up is not the most pleasant of experiences. Bunny had never thought he would need to undergo anything like it in his lifetime. He was not the law-breaking sort! But having damaged the police vehicle sufficiently by falling on it Bunny had apparently committed an adequate degree of crime to end up in the lock-up.

He gathered his wits, realized that the sun was already up and panicked on recalling that he had to reach the international conference venue by 9 am.

He looked for his watch but it was nowhere to be seen. He then recalled that he had seen in films that policemen take away all possessions when one is arrested.

He then noticed a companion in the cell, a short thin scruffy-looking man in jeans and tee shirt.

'Why are you here?' was the man's question.

'I fell on top of a police car. What's the time?' was Bunny's response and counter-question.

'6 o'clock,' was the other's response.

'So why are you here?' was Bunny's second question to him.

'I stole some money from a cop,' was the gentleman's answer.

Both men sighed and nodded as if sighing and nodding were the most natural things to do at the time. They probably were.

Niyati was not one to lose her temper but she was really fuming as she drove Bunny back to the guesthouse.

'How could you! A movie! Just think what would happen if the media gets to know of this! I can already see the headlines, *'Funny Bunny lands in lock-up. Secretary bails him out.'*

Bunny opened his mouth to tell his Secretary that she would probably not figure in the headlines at all, but since he didn't want to annoy her any further he shut it again. In any case his head was still paining from the previous night's blow.

To top it all, the Inspector had given him an earful before allowing him to leave without pressing any charges. Bunny wondered whether the Inspector's children were his fans. Bunny had a great following amongst youngsters after all! Niyati continued to lecture him all the way to the guesthouse. His head kept ringing even after he had showered and readied himself.

She had summoned a doctor to check him up. The elderly gentleman spent about three minutes examining him and declared him fighting fit, even though the spot where he'd received the blow was still aching.

Once the Doctor left, Niyati gave him a pep talk for the first time ever. Her emphasis was upon the fact that Bunny was sky high on the popularity charts and he must capitalize upon that while the going was good. By doing something foolish of the sort he'd done last night his reputation could be ruined forever.

Bunny wanted to tell Niyati that wanting to see a film at night was not a crime and that it had not been his life's ambition to fall atop the police car; it had happened by mistake. But he just nodded and left it at that.

He would mull over his future at the end of the day, he promised himself. He was not sure whether he wanted to be giving speeches for the rest of his life.

International conferences are no different from others except that there is more media spotlight and more security at them. Bunny was frisked a few times before he could enter the venue. After his very recent brush with the law he did not want to annoy any uniformed person. He did not complain even when one guard's hand touched the painful spot behind his ear.

Bunny was the third speaker of the morning session. The first two were internationally renowned ones and the audience was expectant and charged up when his turn came. Niyati looked very nervous but Bunny was sure of himself.

The gorgeous looking emcee introduced him in glowing terms and he wondered whether he should ask for her number then or later. He decided upon the latter.

He marched up to the dais like the seasoned pro that he had become and looked at the audience. He was taken aback to see his parents in the third row. He'd forgotten that they'd promised to be present at the talk.

After smiling at them quickly, he got down to business.

'Ladies and gentlemen, if I tell you that I was in a police lock-up a few hours ago, would you believe me? Would you?'

Most shook their heads and some even shouted 'no' aloud. Niyati held her face and Bunny's parents looked very concerned.

'Stranger things have happened, let me tell you that. There is a need for all of us to be happy with our lot! When was the last time that you thanked God for what you are today and for all the joys he has given you?'

He stopped for a few seconds and gave a few members of the audience telling looks.

'Life is fleeting and the world is too unreal to be taken seriously. Just be happy!'

Bunny was now in true form and the audience, including his folks and Niyati, was suitably impressed.

He carried on in this vein for thirty minutes. It did not matter to him that he was addressing icons and the like. He treated them as if they were his students at the Institute. He made them laugh and he made their eyes moisten. He had them enthralled when he told them of his own story.

'I switched from being a restaurant manager to a multiplex head, from being a banker to a coach, and from a dance instructor to a motivational speaker. And in different cities! I somehow managed to keep my cool at most times, to keep smiling and to take the rough with the smooth without letting either affect me. I have a long way to go but there's one lesson I've learnt pretty early: vendetta and jealousy do not take one far; a sunny attitude to life and to people does!'

Bunny was enjoying himself more than ever. He felt supremely confident. He ended with a flourish and a 'Namaste'.

They went gaga over him. He got a standing ovation. Mr. & Mrs. Kapoor were in tears. Niyati was jumping. People patted him on the back and on the head, with painful results, but he didn't mind.

He was delighted to have brought some smiles into the lives of total strangers. Bunny realised then that what he was doing was worth all the trouble. He would continue to give speeches after all!

His parents were the toast of the media. They had to pose repeatedly with Bunny for the camerapersons.

'Niyati!' Bunny said as she neared the happy family. 'It's all because of you that I was able to bring a glow on the faces of all these people. You deserve all the credit for making me what I am.'

Niyati had tears of joy in her eyes. She had some good news to share too.

'Meet my fiancé, Bhuvanesh Kapoor! We're getting married!' she introduced a balding portly gentleman who looked twice her age.

The man had a gleam in his eye and thrust out a hand towards a bewildered Bunny.

'So you're the imposter!' Bhuvanesh Kapoor said as Bunny shook it shyly, speechless for once. He wondered how he had misjudged Niyati so badly. She must be mad!

Bunny's bean bag felt a lot more comfortable than the prison cell had. As he sank into its depths at the end of the day, he mulled.

He felt more content than he'd felt in a long time. He asked himself if he needed anything else in his life.

'Maybe a new car,' was the answer that he got from within.

He had almost entered the throes of deep sleep when another thought came to his mind.

'Maybe Tarana!'

Bunny was aware that she had returned to Mumbai recently and had landed a job in Delhi. She'd been in touch with him off and on through social networking sites and via email. But they had not spoken to each other in months now.

'Hello! Tarana, this is Bunny! I hope I didn't disturb you at this unearthly hour. I just felt like talking to you...it's been so long!' he whispered into the phone so that his parents wouldn't wake up, but he was loud enough for her to hear.

He heard her sigh loudly in astonishment.

'Bunny...' was all she could say.

The voice at the other end was as musical as it had ever been. She did not need to say anything else immediately. The way she'd said his name was explanation enough.

His pulse raced, as did his thoughts. That indefinite something still existed between them!

The precise moment when Bunny Kapoor fell asleep that night remains unknown to mankind till this day. What is known is that his telephone bill took rapid strides towards infinity.